TRIAL BY

AMBUSH

Legal thrillers by Michael Monhollon

Trial by Ambush (Robin Starling #1)

Juggling Evidence (Robing Starling #2)

Dog Law (Robin Starling #3)

Laughing Heirs (Robin Starling #4)

Devil in the Dock (Robin Starling #5)

Gone Ballistic (Robin Starling #6)

Sexual Misconduct (Robin Starling #7)

Criminal Intent

Guilty Knowledge

A Robin Starling Courtroom Mystery

Book 1

TRIAL BY AMBUSH

Michael Monhollon

Reflection Publishing

Abilene, Texas

For Rachel

Chapter 1

Cynthia Reeves, a pretty if slightly overweight secretary with a corona of blonde hair, stood just inside the door of my office, one hand on the doorknob, tears streaming down her face. I was at my desk, my laptop open on the corner of the desk, a pen in my hand, a legal pad in front of me. As I sat staring at her, I probably looked like a deer caught in the headlights.

"It was so demeaning," she said, gasping between sobs to suck in breath enough to speak. "Nobody's ever talked to me that way before."

I hated to ask. On the other hand, she was in my office for help or sympathy or...Actually, I didn't know what she was there for. Both of us were women. I figured that had something to do with it, even if the lawyer-secretary divide was between us. "Who?" I said. "Who talked to you that way?"

"That Steve Kelley."

One of a dozen associate attorneys, this one a couple of years behind me. "Steve Kelley said something demeaning?"

"He called me..." She paused for a loud sniff,

1

retracting a wad of snot that had blossomed briefly in one nostril. "He called me a fixed unit of labor."

This was one of those moments when I resented the glass wall between my office and the corridor. Even with the door closed, I had nowhere to hide.

"A what?"

"A fixed unit of labor."

I hadn't misheard. "What was this about?"

"Coffee. When he got to work this morning, the pot in the lounge was empty."

Cynthia's desk was probably the one closest to the lounge, which may be the reason she had gotten the first blast of Steve's pique. "So he came running out of the lounge and called you a fixed unit of labor?"

She nodded, red-faced and sniffling. "I've never been called anything like that before." She drew herself up to her full height, which was somewhere around five-four. Her dark skirt and contrasting pastel top made her look shorter—and a bit thick about the middle. "I will not stand for it," she said.

"No, I guess not. He thought you should be monitoring the coffee pot, I take it."

The snot-blossom had reappeared, pulsing distractingly in her right nostril. "Yes. I don't have anything better to do, he said. I'm just a fixed unit of labor."

The pen in my hand began to beat a tattoo against the blotter on my desk. I put it down, pursing my lips to hide the grin I felt tugging at the corners of my mouth. "Do you ever make the coffee?" I asked.

"Sure. If I want some. Or I ask one of the gofers to do it." The gofers evidently being fixed units of labor, even if she were not.

"You're too busy to make a pot around eight-thirty

every morning?" I asked.

Her breasts began heaving, not quite in sync with the throb of the snot-blossom. She was beginning to hyperventilate.

"I'll talk to Steve," I said hastily.

"Tell him he can make other arrangements for his coffee."

"I will." Though, of course, there was no particular reason he should listen to me.

"Thanks, Robin." She opened the door and went out. "Wouldn't hurt him to make a pot himself every once in a while," she muttered as the door swung shut behind her.

I slumped in my chair. Some days it just wasn't worth coming to work, I thought. I took a deep breath and let it out slowly. As I picked up my pen and straightened my shoulders, a woman I hadn't seen in ten years strode past my office. I blinked and looked again.

The woman was still visible through the wall of floor-to-ceiling glass, but all I could see was a tailored suit and the dark mass of hair that fell past her shoulders. She darted a glance over her shoulder as she turned a corner, and I was sure.

It was Wendy Walters, her face beautiful and not much changed, though it was not one to fill me with warm fuzzy feelings. We'd had a falling out over a guy once, a pretty bad falling out...to be entirely forthright, something of a catfight.

I staggered as I got out of my chair to go after her, and, as I recovered my balance, mentally cursed the unaccustomed three-inch heels. What some women will go through to please a man, I thought. By the time I got to the corner, Wendy was nowhere to be seen, but Steve Kelley, that coffee-loving harrier of secretaries, was coming toward me.

"Did you pass a woman just now?" I asked him.

He stopped, frowning slightly in apparent contemplation. "What did she look like?" he asked.

"She looked like a woman. Did you pass one or not?"

"About your height, a lot of dark hair, legs up to here?" He raised his hand, palm down, to the level of his neck. His jacket was off, his sleeves rolled halfway up his forearms to expose a gold wristwatch and thick, blond wrist hair.

He had seen her. "I'm surprised you're not trailing after her with your tongue cleaning lint from the carpet," I said. I turned and headed back toward my office.

"I have some self-control," he called after me. "Otherwise I'd be trailing after you."

I glanced back over my shoulder in time to catch his wink. I rolled my eyes and went through the door into my office, where I dropped into my chair just in time to see Wendy Walters going by again.

"Wendy!" I called as I lurched again to my feet on those treacherous heels. Why I'd let John Parker talk me into wearing heels to work was beyond me.

Wendy's shoulders hunched as she turned her head, but they relaxed when she saw me. "Robin," she said, coming to the door. "I was looking for you."

Not so I could tell it. "It looked as though you were trying to get away from someone."

Her eyes darted left and came back to me. "That, too. You got a minute?"

"Sure. Come in and have a seat."

She hesitated in the doorway. "The last time I saw you, I believe I slapped your face," she said.

I allowed one corner of my mouth to rise as I sat behind my desk. "No, you tried to slap me, but missed. So you spit on me."

"Gross. You sure?"

"You don't forget a loogie like that one."

"I almost feel like I should apologize." She sat, finally, in one of the client chairs and tugged at a skirt that was really too short for office wear.

"Don't apologize," I said, waving it off. "I had it coming."

"That's true. You knew Cody and I were together."

Cody. That was his name.

Her gaze slipped past me to the framed diplomas and law license hanging on the wall behind me, then returned to meet mine. "And I found you in the gym with your tongue down his throat," she said. "It almost broke us up, you know."

Even at the age of thirty, it was hard for me to remember a passion so great that when it had swept over me in a gymnasium hallway, its current was all but irresistible.

"You're still together?" I asked.

"No. I guess it did break us up eventually. At least it was a precipitating factor. Hard to believe, isn't it? One kiss."

I felt my lip curl. "Is that all he admitted to? The kiss you caught him at?"

She studied me a moment. "Crap," she said. "And I believed him. You slept with him, didn't you?"

I shrugged uncomfortably. "Men are such liars," I offered.

5

"I'll give you that."

I said, "If it makes you feel any better, I felt really guilty about it for a really long time." Still felt guilty, if it came to that. What do you do with guilt, other than wait for it to fade? I thought it had faded, but after ten years, here it was, buried deep but solid as bedrock. "What ever happened to Cody anyway?"

"Last I heard he was coaching middle school football down in Blacksburg. That was a while back."

"What are you doing now?"

"Accounting."

"Ah," I said. She'd been an accounting major when I'd known her.

"I saw your name in the paper a few months ago," she said.

Double-Ah. I'd wondered to what I owed the pleasure.

"It was quite a piece. Robin Starling, taking on the tobacco industry," she said.

"Not exactly. Representing one tobacco company and suing another."

"Playing with the big boys, though. How long have you been doing it?"

"I've been in commercial litigation six years. Give or take."

She nodded.

"I didn't even know you were in Richmond," I said.

"I started off in Alexandria. I've been back three years now."

I waited. She took a breath and looked back over her shoulder. "Do you mind?" She gestured toward the door.

"No, go ahead."

"Thank you." She went to the door and shut it, then came back and pulled the client chair closer to the desk.

It was all beginning to seem a little weird to me. "Are you okay?" I asked.

She moved her head equivocally, the overhead fluorescents glinting in her dark brown hair. She'd always had nice hair. I myself have straight blonde hair without a lot of body, and hair envy comes naturally to me.

She opened her mouth, then hesitated. "Can we go somewhere? I don't want to talk here," she said.

"It's the glass walls. They take some getting used to, but no one can hear us."

She looked through the floor-to-ceiling glass into the interior hallway and did not seem reassured. I didn't blame her. There's something psychologically oppressive about doing business in a fishbowl. The partners of the firm have offices along the outer wall of the building with solid interior walls and exterior walls of floor-to-ceiling glass and spectacular views of the city or the James River. We associates have offices in the interior of the building, and they all have glass walls.

"It's worse than you think," I said. "The overhead lights are motion-sensitive. If you fall asleep at your desk, they go out." I smiled. "Don't ask me how I know."

Her mouth twitched, but not in response to anything I was saying. Her breathing was getting rapid and shallow as her eyes tracked one of our gofers who was walking down the hall with a manila envelope in one hand and a diet Coke in the other. He looked in at us as he went by, turning his head further and further as he walked. Fortunately for him, he passed out of sight before his neck snapped.

"He can't hear us," I said.

"I've seen him before." Her tongue passed over her lips, and she continued more strongly, "Downstairs, when I was getting on the elevator. He was watching me."

I laughed. "Horny Hal?"

"What?"

"His name is actually Harold Hornsby, but if he tries to stand close to you when you're wearing a dress, you want to check the tops of his shoes for mirrors."

"So you think…"

"I think you in that outfit would draw Harold's gaze like a magnet draws steel."

She smiled, but only faintly. Her mouth opened as if she was going to say something, but she closed it again as her gaze went back to the empty hallway.

"We could go down to the food court," I suggested. "Have a latte or something."

She shook her head. "I really don't want to be seen with you."

That set me back. "I could freshen my makeup. Fix my lipstick or whatever."

"You're okay. I don't want to put either of us in danger, that's all."

The paranoia was beginning to freak me out. "We can find us an out-of-the-way corner to sit and talk," I said. "Let's go down." I stood and reached for my purse.

"Is there a back stairway or something? I don't think I was followed, but just in case someone is watching the elevators…"

"Sure. We can use the back stairs."

We passed John Parker on our way past the elevators. Another one of the firm's associate attorneys, but good-looking enough to grace the cover of GQ, he was the man responsible for the most uncomfortable pair of shoes I could remember ever wearing. He was coming back from somewhere with a leather portfolio tucked under his arm, and his eyes cut automatically to Wendy's legs, his eyebrows lifting appreciatively.

The son of a gun. John had been dating me the past nine months and sleeping with me for three, and he had me teetering around in a pair of pumps that was supposed to make me look statuesque, but probably, given my height, made me look Amazonian. I planted a heel on his instep as we went by him and grimaced in satisfaction when I heard the swift intake of breath. When I looked back at him as we turned the corner, he gave me a wince and a shrug that I took to be an apology.

Magnanimously, I nodded my forgiveness.

Chapter 2

By the time we reached the bottom of nine flights of stairs, I was about ready to chuck the pumps and go barefoot, but I restrained myself. Eventually, we got to the fire door that opened into the food court. Wendy pushed it open an inch or two and stood looking out through the crack.

"What do you see?" I asked her.

"There's a security guard by the elevators."

"Black guy in uniform? That's normal. He's supposed to be there."

There was a distant ding. "People are getting off one of the elevators. Now people are getting on."

Not what I would call a newsflash. "Anyone just hanging around keeping an eye on things?"

"No."

"Let's go then."

She took a breath and let it out. Then she pushed through the fire door, and I followed her, trying not to wobble. When I realized she was heading for the main doors, I shook my head in exasperation. In a few strides I caught up to her. "Look," I said. "These are new shoes, and my feet are killing me. Let's get a coffee or something and sit for a minute."

She stopped at the corner of a shop, her head still, her eyes moving.

"Over here," I said encouragingly, taking a couple of steps toward the coffee shop.

"I don't drink coffee."

"That's all right. They've got smoothies and all sorts of other stuff. Let's get something cold."

"Okay."

In deference to our waistlines, which we both wanted to keep, Wendy and I got smoothies made with nothing but frozen fruit and almond milk. We sat at a table that was shielded by the fountain, where water slid smoothly down the faces of three black stone monoliths. It was past time for breakfast and too early for lunch, so only a scattering of people occupied the tables. Wendy sat with her back to a chrome railing that had nothing but a few plants and a wall behind it, her gaze directed over my shoulder. I glanced back once or twice and saw a person or two sitting or moving about in the wedge that was all that was left of my field of vision: Two old men in windbreakers, a young man in a shirt with an open collar and a sports jacket, a woman popping gum at the counter in the newsstand. Leaning on the railing of the floor above us were a man and a woman, talking and gesturing, each looking angry enough to send the other into free-fall with a quick shove.

I took a sip of my smoothie as I turned back to Wendy. "I don't see him."

"Who?"

"Horny Hal. Anyone else taking an interest."

She nodded reluctantly. "No. I'm just being

paranoid, I guess. I'm pretty sure I wasn't followed here."

"Good. Being followed is bad." I nodded agreeably at her, taking in the tight mouth and the flared nostrils. At that moment, she hardly resembled the girl I'd known a decade ago. "It's been awhile," I said neutrally. In college she and I had played basketball together on one of the top Division III teams in the country. Our senior year took us all the way to the Final Four, where we lost in the semifinal by a single point. Wendy and I held each other and cried. A week later, she stumbled across Cody and me.

"I went with Ernst and Young after I graduated," Wendy said. "You probably knew that."

I probably had at one point, but I had long since forgotten. While Wendy had been majoring in accounting, I myself had majored in English. It was one reason I'd gone to law school. It's hard to find a job with an undergraduate degree in English literature, I'd found.

"After three years with Ernst and Young, I moved over to Krebs-Mueller," Wendy said.

"Pharmaceuticals?"

"Then McCormack Labs acquired Krebs four years ago."

"So now you're with McCormack."

She nodded.

"Big outfit," I said.

"Yes. Krebs isn't the only firm it's acquired. Four years ago, it was just starting on its buying binge. Here. I want you to look at this." She held out her hand, palm downward, only partially concealing a CD in a plastic case.

I took it, then turned my hand over to examine what she had given me.

"Put it away, will you?" she said in a low, fierce voice.

I glanced over my shoulder as I palmed the CD, but the two old geezers having coffee a couple of tables away just didn't look threatening, at least not to me.

"Taylor Swift?" I said conspiratorially.

"Don't be an idiot," she said. "It isn't Taylor Swift."

"Sorry. I was fooled by the mass of blonde hair." I slipped the CD into my purse and lowered the purse to the floor between my feet. "Maybe you ought to tell me what this is about."

"I'm getting to that."

"Okay."

"There are accounting irregularities at McCormack," she said.

I nodded encouragingly, but she had frozen, her lips parted, her gaze fixed on something behind me. Before I could turn, a voice in my ear said, "Hello, ladies."

I exhaled. "Hello, John," I said.

He hooked the leg of a chair with one foot and pulled it out. His eyes were on Wendy as he sat down. "I don't believe we've met," he said. "I'm John Parker."

Wendy's eyes cut to me.

I said, "Her name's Wendy. She and I went to college together."

"Wendy..." His eyes left her face for the instant required to check out her cleavage. I myself had given up deep-V or even scoop necklines, thinking it more professional to deal with other lawyers eye-to-eye rather than boob-to-eye.

Wendy said, "If I give you my last name, are you going to look me up?"

"He'd better not," I said.

She looked at me. "You two are dating?"

"Hard to believe, isn't it?"

John said, "Oozing charm from every pore, he oiled his way across the floor. I'm sorry, I'm intruding." He stood. "Pleased to meet you, Wendy. Robin." He gave me a whimsical smile, then nodded and strode off across the food court. Wendy and I looked after him.

"He'd be unbearably smarmy if he weren't such a fox," she said. "Sorry, I shouldn't insult your boyfriend."

"He's not usually like that. It's the sight of a nice rack and a tight bod that does it to him."

"A nice rack and a tight bod?"

"Guy talk," I said. "I work in a law office that's ninety percent male."

"You'd think that would be a good thing," she said.

"You would, wouldn't you?"

Wendy took a sip of her drink and stood. "I can't talk here. Let's take a walk."

I took a breath and released it in capitulation. "Okay," I said, and I squelched the throb of protest from my toes.

When we were out on the street, I said, "You were going to tell me about accounting irregularities at McCormack."

She didn't answer. A fifty-year-old man in a blue

blazer went past us, walking purposefully.

"Well?" I said.

Wendy glanced back, but the sidewalk was clear for a block behind us. "I guess I'd better start with a little background."

"Okay."

"McCormack Labs has contractual relationships with a bunch of little R&D outfits—joint ventures, partnerships, all kinds of things."

I nodded. Any pharmaceutical company would need a lot of research and development.

"A lot of them involve people who used to work for McCormack, who left to develop ideas of their own. McCormack's got fifty or sixty attorneys in its legal department. Once upon a time, when engineers and research scientists tried to leave the company with ideas they'd come up with, McCormack would sue them for running off with its intellectual property. Now McCormack's lawyers structure deals with them and draw up contracts. McCormack settles for a piece of the action."

"Uh huh," I said.

She waited for a gaggle of women to pass us, all of them honking merrily. "Many of the transactions haven't been arms-length," Wendy said when the laughter had faded behind us. "The companies are related to McCormack in some way, to McCormack or to one or more of its officers."

"That's pretty common, isn't it? You just said a lot of them used to work for McCormack."

"The deals can be too cozy. Having control of multiple entities allows McCormack to apportion profits and losses to suit itself. It opens the door for some really aggressive earnings management."

15

"As opposed to some really passive earnings management?" I said.

She didn't see the humor in my question, and maybe there wasn't any. She said, "A little earnings management used to be considered legitimate. A company that could avoid big swings in reported earnings would have a stock price that was less volatile. The SEC used to give them a little leeway."

"Before Enron," I said.

"Enron and WorldCom and Sunbeam and all the rest of them—a whole host of companies doing everything they could to hide losses and debt and to exaggerate earnings, hoping that a booming market would bail them out in a year or two. In the meantime, investors were making their decisions based on phony financials."

"McCormack Labs has been able to do all this despite Sarbanes-Oxley?" Sarbanes-Oxley was the federal legislation designed to put an end to such accounting shenanigans.

"Sarb-Ox raised the stakes. It didn't change human nature."

"Touché."

A man and a much younger woman were coming up behind us, talking animatedly. Wendy stopped, and I stopped with her. We stood against a building that had a men's clothing store on the first floor until the couple had passed.

"She's his mistress," I said.

"You know them?"

"If they were married they wouldn't have anywhere near that much to say to each other. Sorry—you were just getting to securities fraud."

Wendy took a step and tossed her smoothie into

the trashcan by the curb. "McCormack has always pushed the envelope," she said. "As of a year or so ago, its stock price had doubled every couple of years over a ten year period. McCormack used the inflated stock as security to finance many of its deals. Of course, lately its stock price has been under pressure."

"Everybody's stock price has been under pressure." Despite continuing contributions, my own 401(k) was no higher than it had been two years ago.

"Yes, but some companies are especially vulnerable, McCormack among them. It's down maybe twenty-five percent over the past year, and it can't take much more. If the price of its stock fails to stabilize, many of its deals are going to collapse. A big drop in its stock price could destroy the company. I guess you see where this is taking us."

I didn't, not clearly, so I said, "You're saying McCormack has to keep manipulating earnings to keep its stock price up."

"Yes, and it can't afford even the breath of a scandal."

I started moving again, and, as Wendy followed, I said, "Have you talked to anyone about it? What do the other people in accounting say?"

Wendy's mouth twisted. "The first time I questioned the way we were reporting something, the controller gave me the Loyalty Speech."

"Yours is not to reason why..."

"Exactly. The next time, I put my concerns more forcefully, and he gave me the Chicken Little speech. The company is doing well because of the deals it's put together, and it has top people structuring those deals. Don't go around talking about the sky falling."

"But you think it may be."

"The controller does too. He has to. Of course, in the meantime he's getting rich off it."

"So what's on the CD you gave me?"

Wendy stepped against me to avoid the mailbox at the corner, and I felt the gooseflesh on her arm when it brushed against mine. It was August, and, though we were not yet in the heat of the day, I myself was beginning to sweat. Wendy stopped. "Excel files," she said softly. "I think I've discovered a second set of books."

I inclined my head toward her. "A what?"

"I think the company's keeping two sets of accounting records, which means that McCormack's reported earnings aren't just exaggerated. They're completely fictional."

"So it's not a matter of distorted judgment here and there…"

"No. It's systematic fraud."

"And somebody's going to jail."

"Some rich, powerful somebodies."

"Who have you told?"

"I don't know who to tell. If what I've uncovered really are two sets of books, then the fraud goes all the way to the top. The outside auditors may be implicated."

Chapter 3

Wendy had to get back to work before she was missed, she said. We headed back toward my office, but Wendy stopped us while we were still a couple of blocks away.

"It would be better if we split up here," she said.

"If you say so."

The paranoid touches seemed overwrought, but even paranoids have enemies. Wendy was in a position to have a better understanding of the situation than I did.

"Do you think you could circle around and approach your building from another direction?"

"Not in these shoes," I said.

She looked down at them. "They're cute," she said. "Give you almost a feminine look."

"Careful."

She laughed, for the moment more normal than she'd been since appearing in my office. "I'm sorry. Can you wait five minutes then? I'm parked right up the street. I can get away, and no one who might be hanging around will know we're together."

I took a breath, released it. "Okay," I said.

She walked along the sidewalk, uphill and then down and out of sight. Obeying instructions has never been one of my strong suits. I counted to ten and then followed. When I caught sight of her, she was a block-and-a-half away. The headlights of a cherry red convertible beeped as she approached it. Her pace quickened as a man started getting out of an Audi two cars behind hers. He had a day's growth of beard and black, close-cropped hair.

I quickened my pace, too, but the man dropped back into his car even as Wendy was opening the door and swinging down into hers. My next thought was that he was going to follow her, but her car pulled away from the curb, drawing a honk from a minivan that had to slow down abruptly to keep from hitting her, and the Audi continued to sit there. As I got closer, I could see that the man was talking on his cell phone.

I turned my head, but Wendy had already turned the corner. She was gone.

That was fine. I had her files to look at.

Unfortunately, as I had learned from the moment I entered legal practice, associate attorneys don't always have control over their own time. When I got to my office, the phone's message light was on. The message was, "Yo! Starling! My office pronto." The voice didn't identify itself, but it belonged to Eric Beezer, one of the firm's junior partners. I had forgotten I was supposed to help him on a brief he was writing. I sighed, slung my purse into the kneehole of my desk, then headed for Beezer's office.

Eric Beezer had an office with walls, but the door was open, showing Beezer sprawled on his back across his desk, one foot touching the floor, the other trailing about six inches above it. The floor to ceiling window beyond him looked out over the city of Richmond, Virginia.

"Eric?" I said tentatively.

"Come in, Starling." He didn't turn his head as I entered the office, or even open his eyes. "It's there on the computer. You can take the chair."

Several inches of one leg were visible above the sock, and his shirt had pulled out of the waistband of his slacks. As I went around the desk, I glanced at the soft, milky belly thatched with dark hair. About fifty pounds overweight, Beezer looked as if the tide had gone out and left him beached atop his desk.

The desk chair squeaked as I took a seat in front of the computer on the credenza.

"Okay, read me what I've got so far." His face was turned upward toward the ceiling.

I looked at the screen. "Starting with the first point of error?"

"Sure. Start with that."

I read it to him. The writing was rough, evidently transcribed from dictation and not yet proofread. After a sentence or two, I said, "Hold on. Subject-verb agreement." I corrected it, went on. On the second page was something that should have been part of the first paragraph. I stopped talking while I moved it. "None of these citations is formatted correctly."

"So fix them," he said.

"Do you need to be here?" I asked. "Am I keeping you from something?"

"Good point." He heaved himself into sitting position and looked blearily at me. "You're a fox, you know that, Starling? A cold, stone fox."

"Yes, thank you. Does Mrs. Beezer think so, too?"

"Another good point. You're full of them today." He surged to his feet. "So I should check on your progress in, what, a couple hours?"

"It's nearly lunch time."

"Okay, fine. Let's say midafternoon."

"Three o'clock?"

"Sure, if that works for you. You know why I cut you so much slack, Starling?"

"I'm afraid I do."

"Yes, you're a smart girl." He gestured at my feet. "Like the shoes," he said.

"I understand they make me look feminine."

"No one would ever mistake you for a boy, that's for sure." He shook his head as he lumbered out of the office. "That's for sure." When he had disappeared from sight, I turned back to his computer.

Well, crap, I thought. I didn't see any reason to sit in his office and do this, so I fished out the flash drive that hung on the lanyard beneath my blouse. After I'd saved his document to it, I headed back to my own office, stopping on the way to make myself an almond butter sandwich from the materials I kept in the break room refrigerator.

I ate the sandwich at my desk while I tried to flesh out Beezer's half-baked ideas and sort out the tangled legal references in his brief. I emailed it to Beezer at a quarter to three and padded down to the break room in my bare feet to get a bottle of water.

Cynthia followed me in.

"Did you get a chance to…"

I shook my head at her. "I'm sorry. I haven't yet."

"I appreciate you taking me seriously," she said.

I nodded wearily, reaching into the refrigerator. I took my water bottle to the leather sofa and plopped down on it. "You know, this isn't really the best work environment for a woman," I said. "Here you're a fixed unit of labor who should be keeping the coffee pot full. You get suggestive comments; they look you up and down...None of them have pawed at you, have they?"

She shook her head. "I found a dirty limerick written on my desk blotter one morning last week. I don't know who wrote it. 'There once was a man from Kent...'"

I waved her silent. "I know it," I said. "It's been on my blotter, too."

Pete Larsen, the managing partner, came in. Cynthia gave him a quick nod and skedaddled. As he opened the refrigerator and peered into it, I sat up straighter on the couch. I got a frown from him anyway as he turned away from the fridge. I thought it was the bare feet, but he said, "We don't encourage the staff to use this lounge, you know, Ms. Starling."

The coffee pot began to sputter, just finishing its brewing cycle. Evidently, someone had set it before Cynthia and I came in. I looked at it, then back at Larsen.

"I'm sorry," I said. "I'd just asked her to make a pot of coffee."

His face cleared. "Oh. That's all right then." His mouth stretched in what might have been a smile.

He left, and I sat sipping my water for maybe thirty minutes, needing the break, though I couldn't imagine who I was going to bill the time to. When I got back to my office, Eric Beezer was waiting for me. I stopped and let my head roll back.

"You've done some good work here, Starling."

I sighed as I stood looking at him.

"Without you around, I'd have to devote a lot more care to this sort of thing." He smiled, but his smile made him look as if he were passing a kidney stone. "That's what I think of as the doomsday scenario."

"Glad I could help." I started toward my desk.

"Still, there're a few things that require a bit more work." He riffled the printout at me as I passed him, and I could see what was surely, given the short time he'd had the brief, an excessive number of corrections scrawled in green ink.

"Okay." I dropped into my chair, took the papers from him.

"You're an asset to the firm," he said. "I hear people say it all the time."

I waited.

"What?" he said. "Oh, *asset*. You're expecting some sort of pun. No, the word just came out. I didn't have anything in mind." He paused in the doorway and opened his mouth to say something.

"Don't," I said. "You're doing so well."

He closed his mouth again, gave me a shrug and a sheepish grin. Then he was gone.

It was nearly six when I finished with his brief again, and I was beat. I emailed the file to Beezer, got my briefcase, and went to find John Parker.

John was gone, though, and his office was dark behind the glass walls. I frowned. He hadn't even looked in on me before he left, which wasn't like him. And me with my new shoes and flexed calves.

Several other lawyers got on the elevator with me, one of them Steve Kelley, the man who saw

24

secretaries as fixed units of labor. He had an office near John's, so I asked him what time John had left.

One of Steve's eyebrows went up, but he shook his head. "I haven't seen John since mid-afternoon sometime."

"He borrowed my dictionary and never gave it back to me," I said. It was untrue, but John and I had agreed to keep our relationship low-key, if not quite secret.

"Unh huh," Steve said. He exchanged a look with one of the other lawyers.

"What do you mean, unh huh?"

Steve winked at me.

"What?" I said.

"Nothing. I haven't seen John, and I don't know anything about a dictionary." There was a snort behind me, and I spun on a first-year associate named Matt, who went immediately stiff.

"Why should you know anything about my dictionary?" I said to Steve.

Steve gave me a knowing smile, and I considered whacking him with my purse. The elevator doors slid open on the lobby floor, though, and I flipped my pony tail at all of them and stalked out. There was a brief burst of laughter behind me, quickly muffled.

If John Parker's big yap had made me the subject of office gossip, then he had a lot to answer for. I didn't want to share another elevator cab with Steve and company when we got to the parking garage, so I quickened my pace, my heels clacking on the tile as I strode past the black monoliths with their falling water.

On the far side of the lobby, I entered a short hall and slipped between the closing doors of the elevator.

Two people were there before me, a man and a woman, but I didn't know either one of them. The man got off with me on level four and walked beside me in the direction of my car.

I glanced at him. He was wearing a polo shirt and needed a shave, and there was something familiar about him. I stopped at my car, a VW Beetle, and he glanced at it as he went past. He didn't get into a car himself, but turned up the ramp to the next level.

I frowned, shrugged, opened my car door and tossed my briefcase and my purse across onto the passenger seat.

Chapter 4

I carried my shoes into the house and, as soon as I got to the bedroom, tossed them into the closet and shrugged out of my dress. The bra I'd been wearing still smelled like laundry soap, so I put it back in the drawer and got out an exercise bra to replace it. After pulling on a T-shirt and a pair of gym shorts, I grabbed my running shoes and a pair of balled socks and padded barefoot to the kitchen.

I was going to exercise, but not until after I'd eaten. I run better if I eat something first, as long as I don't eat too much or run too hard. I dumped some salad from a bag in the vegetable drawer into a bowl, sliced in a leftover chicken breast, and sprinkled on a little raspberry vinaigrette. I ate in front of the TV, watching American Idol on the DVR. Somehow, I never get to watch it at the same time as the rest of the country.

When I was done eating, I let a commercial run while I washed my dish and fork and laid them on a dishcloth to dry. Then I went back into the living room to do my stretches while American Idol finished up. It was beginning to get dark when I set out on my nightly run, a five-mile loop through Richmond's far west end.

Nine months ago, when I started dating John Parker, I'd adjusted my run to pass through the apartment complex where he lived. He didn't know I ran past his building four nights a week, though, and I didn't plan to tell him. It would make me look weird.

Thirty minutes into the run, I was trotting down the unevenly lighted sidewalk that bisected his apartment complex. John's car wasn't in his parking space, so I knew he wasn't home. Still, as I went by it, I glanced up at the balcony of John's second-floor apartment. Pure habit.

The French doors stood open, beyond them a glow of shifting, bluish light. The television, I thought. Maybe John had had car trouble, but was home now watching television. I heard a woman speaking—no surprise—but I came to a stop with a little stutter-step as I realized that the voice was live rather than televised.

John had a girl up there, and the girl wasn't me. That wasn't right. I stood there on the sidewalk, breathing hard, feeling numb, having no idea what to do. For perhaps a minute I did nothing at all. Then I came to myself.

With a quick, furtive glance about me to make sure I was unobserved, I moved off the sidewalk and against the wall of John's building where I stood next to the privacy fence that circled the patio of the apartment below his. Other than the indistinct murmur of the television, no sound came from above me.

After a half-minute or so, I allowed myself to breathe again, trying to relax. *Maybe you imagined the voice*, I told myself. *Besides, the reason for running past his apartment has nothing to do with keeping tabs on him. You're just a weird chick who has to run somewhere, why not somewhere that interests you? Just go on with your run. Accept what you heard, or think you heard, as the subject of future rumination, and go on.*

So persuasive an advocate am I, at least when talking to myself, that my right leg actually gave a twitch in the direction of home. My left leg, though— my left leg just wasn't going to go along. Ah well. So much for not keeping tabs.

I glanced across at the building opposite and didn't see anyone, then went up on my toes to peek over the six-foot privacy fence I was standing next to. At five-eleven, I'm used to seeing over things. Inside the fence, the patio was vacant but for the dark shapes of a lounge chair and a gas grill.

What I was about to do is no doubt evidence of one of the less pleasant aspects of my personality: curiosity combined with a lack of respect for the privacy of others. If I wanted to know about something or someone—and if no one was ever going to know that I knew—then I could satisfy my curiosity, and no one's sense of privacy would be violated: Their privacy, okay; their *sense* of privacy, no. If that strikes you as a distinction without a difference, you have to realize there's some expensive legal training at work here.

I put my hands on the ledger board that ran along the top of the privacy fence. With a hop and a push, I got one foot onto the top of the fence, then the other, and I stood with one palm just brushing the brick wall of the building for balance. As I straightened, my left knee popped. It had been doing that lately. I'd turned thirty last fall, and with that milestone came this audible indicator of my mortality.

From the fence I could see into John's galley-style kitchen, but there was no one there. I stretched upward on my toes so I could grasp the square metal uprights of John's balcony railing as high as possible, then swung a sneakered foot up between two of the uprights. I pulled myself up, swung one leg over the railing, then the other. On the balcony, working to keep my breathing quiet, I stepped around the wrought-iron love seat to the wall beside the open French doors.

No voices were coming from the apartment any longer, not even from the TV, but I could hear breathing—then a grunt and the creaking of the living room sofa. I mouthed a silent curse. There was no question in my mind as to what John and his female companion were doing. Only two nights ago, John had been in there doing it with me, which made him a pig. I wasn't sure what it made me.

I crouched, one hand on the jamb of the door for balance, then took my peek, leaning in and out in a single swaying motion. I saw long, dark hair, his open hands against the pale skin of her back, tangled clothes...and the image became an afterimage, a ghost on my retina as I put my forehead against the brick wall beside the open doors. The pain I felt was like a blow to the solar plexus, paralyzing my diaphragm so that I couldn't draw air.

In the apartment building opposite, a dog started barking. As if in answer, a small yelp sounded inside John's apartment, and the sound of movement followed. "There's someone out there," a woman said urgently, and somehow I managed to move. I stepped up onto the balcony railing, bracing myself against the overhanging eave.

"There's no one out there." John's voice.

"That dog's barking at something. Go look."

A schnauzer was on the balcony of the apartment opposite to John's. It locked eyes with me and began barking in earnest, bracing its paws on the balcony railing. It wasn't going to stop. Behind me, someone was coming. I took a breath and stepped off into space. The dark ground rushed toward me. My feet hit, the weight of my fall driving me down onto my hands and knees. The air in my lungs gusted out of me, but I pushed at the ground with feet and hands, forcing myself upright.

I staggered toward John's building and wedged myself behind the close-packed branches of a rhododendron. John came out onto the balcony, his hands holding up his pants, and the dog stopped barking. Little fur-ball.

"What is it? Who do you see?" Something about the woman's voice was beginning to disturb me.

"There's no one," John said.

She stepped through the doorway beside him, still buttoning her blouse, and, of course, I knew her. It was Wendy Walters. It had taken her ten years to do it, but the little tramp had finally gotten back at me. She looked around carefully, not taking John's word as to what was where. Her eyes focused on the shadowy movements of the rhododendron, and it seemed to me for a moment that our eyes met. I held my breath, having no desire to confront the two of them. I was ashamed—ashamed not only of spying, but of being cheated on, which made no sense at all.

The schnauzer gave a yip.

31

"It's a dog," Wendy said.

"Sure. Just a dog," John agreed.

I exhaled, softly. The drop had shaken me, and my feet stung, but I kept them still.

"I could have sworn it was barking *at* someone, you know?" Wendy said.

"What are you so jumpy about? No one can possibly know you're here."

"I'm not jumpy. It's just the way that dog was barking."

"What difference does it make how the dog was barking? We're on the second floor. It's not like anyone could see anything from the sidewalk." He turned back into the apartment, a hand on her arm by way of encouragement. Clearly, he was ready to get back to what they'd been doing,

Go, go, I thought at her, doing my best to beam my own encouragement telepathically. *Go play some more hanky-panky with my boyfriend, you backstabbing slut.*

They went. I moved my head, stretching the muscles in my neck, still stiff from the fall, but before I could get too relaxed, an outer door whooshed open just around the corner.

"Wendy!" John's voice held exasperation. I slipped out from behind the rhododendron and swiftly skirted the privacy fence, keeping my head down, and ran back down the sidewalk the way I had come.

Nine months with John, that's all it was, I told myself as I circled the apartment complex. No great investment of my life. A little fun, a few laughs…But as I ran along a curving suburban street in the general direction of home, tears kept welling in my eyes, blurring my vision. I wiped them away with the heels of my hands. No great loss, I told myself. I'd had serious boyfriends before, perhaps a dozen of them. John was only the latest. A few months from now and I could be on to boyfriend number thirteen.

How I would miss him, though—miss him, even though I would be seeing him every day at the office.

In a doomed effort to escape the pain, I ran faster and faster, rhythmically cursing in time with my footsteps, the wind in my ears amplified to a dull roaring. Another piece of me torn away and stapled to some guy's bedpost.

When I turned onto my own street, my T-shirt was so wet with perspiration it was sticking to me, and I was blowing like a horse after a long gallop. I didn't notice the car parked across from my house.

I dropped into a walk and continued past my sidewalk. After a hard workout it takes a minute or two for the heart to slow, and, until it stops pumping out the blood at such high volume, your circulatory system needs the help of the leg muscles to send the blood back up to the heart; hence the cool-down. I was in need of an emotional cool-down as well, and I was working on it. *You're better now*, I told myself as I walked. *You're going to be okay.* I got to the corner and turned back toward home.

It was only then that I noticed the silhouette of a man leaning against the low-slung car. I wasn't alarmed, merely uneasy, but my pace slowed. The end of a cigarette glowed orange as the man took a drag from it, then the glow arched away from him as he flicked the cigarette away.

As I drew even with him, he said the last thing I expected to hear from him. He said my name. "Robin Starling?" He had some kind of accent, and his voice was unfamiliar to me. At the edge of my vision, another man was getting out of the car on the passenger side.

I didn't wait to find out what they wanted. I bolted, turning back the way I had come. The hand that was already reaching for me closed on the shoulder of my T-shirt, but by that time I was moving, and I tore loose, already gaining momentum while the man's weight was shifting to bring that first foot forward. By the time you could say he was running, I was halfway to the corner, and the other man was a couple of steps behind the first one.

Chapter 5

In general, you would expect a man to be able to outrun a woman: The average man has longer legs and greater muscle-mass than the average woman. The same holds true at all levels of athletic competition. You'd expect the men's high school basketball team to beat the women's team. In track and field, you'd expect the men to hold the fastest times in all the races, and, with rare exception, you'd be right.

The averages, however, are only modest predictors of the outcome of a contest between any two individuals. At five-eleven, I was an inch or two taller than the average male. I was a natural athlete, and I was in shape. The man who had accosted me was, to all appearances, an average male: roughly my height, maybe five to ten years older, a good bit heavier. Thus, it surprised and terrified me to find that he was gaining on me, that, as I reached the corner of the first cross street, the sound of his breathing was as loud in my ears as the sound of my own. I felt his hand at the nape of my neck, grasping for my ponytail, for a grip on my shirt or my shoulder. I was less than a second away from capture when I pulled the only trick I could think of: I dropped into a crouch, my momentum driving me forward onto my palms and one knee as the shin and then the opposite foot of my pursuer hit my back and passed over. I staggered, gaining my feet even as he drove face-first into the pavement, his up-stretched hands extended above his head, his elbows only partially taking the force of the fall. Sidestepping him, it took me a few steps to regain my speed, and the second pursuer would have gotten me if he had been right behind the first, but he wasn't. The engine of the car in front of my house roared into life, and I glanced over my shoulder as the car's headlights stabbed on and raked my house in a tight turn.

If I'd had some hopes of outrunning two men, I had none of outrunning the car. I turned onto the cross street, now running full out, my mind racing ahead to the choices that were already on me. As my shadow leaped onto the pavement in front of me, cast by the headlights of the skidding car, I turned left into a paved alley. Big trash canisters stood like sentinels on either side, shadowed by backyard trees that overgrew the privacy fences. In the middle of the block, one of the fences was chain-link rather than wood, the twists of wire along the top sticking upward in little spikes that extended just past the top bar. A couple of them tore at my wrist as I reached out, seeking the half-seen bar without breaking stride. Light splashed into the alley behind me as I brought my hand down to grip the bar and jumped, twisting toward and over the fence, one spike raking the inside of my forearm as I went over.

I landed on my butt in something soft, grass and

dust rising around me in an invisible cloud. The sick, sweet smell of decaying compost was momentarily overpowering, and I rolled onto one elbow, gasping in an effort to catch my breath. The alley brightened as the headlights slid closer. I couldn't imagine who these people were, or why they were pursuing me. What had I done to piss them off?

The car stopped just on the other side of the chain-link fence, the sound of its engine low and as smooth as satin. The window on my side of the car was open, but the driver was in shadow.

"I got you, Robin."

There was my name again.

"My pistol is pointed at you," the man said. "Do not make me shoot you." He didn't sound as if it mattered much to him one way or the other.

I pushed onto my hands and feet. "What do you want?" I called, and I coughed as I inhaled a throat full of grass and dust. There was an answering cough, not a human one, but something like the sound of steam chuffing through a pressure valve.

I lurched upward as if it were a starter's pistol, tearing through the trees and the shrubbery at the edge of the lawn before shifting course into the more open ground in the middle. Behind me, a car door slammed. Almost as if the sound had triggered them, the gopher heads of a sprinkler system sprang up around me, one burst of water soaking the left side of my shirt, and, on my next stride, another burst of water hitting me in the face from the right. I kept going.

After ducking and dodging for fifteen minutes or an hour, I climbed a stack of firewood and dropped down into another backyard, this one surrounded by an eight-foot-high privacy fence. For the moment I was alone, which was a relief. Out there, every pair of headlights and every moving shadow had been a threat. In here...but almost immediately I heard footsteps in the driveway. My heart rate quickened almost before it had begun to slow, and I moved away from the fence, looking for a way out. A small, cinder-block tool shed was at the back of the yard, and I ran toward it, my elbow pressed to the stitch in my side. There was a gate behind the shed, and I felt a surge of hope before I noticed the padlock. I looked up, measuring the fence with my eyes, but I'd tear both it and me apart if I tried to climb it.

I turned back, looking for a possible weapon. The knob on the door of the tool shed turned, but the wood had swollen enough so that the door screeched against a crooked threshold that slid with the door as I jerked it open. Glancing toward the front of the yard, I didn't see anyone, but an army could be on the other side of the privacy fence and I wouldn't know it.

It was dark in the tool shed. I raked my forearm along the wall by the door, but if there was a light switch, I failed to find it. My groping hand closed on a pole leaning against the wall, something heavy on the end. A shovel maybe. Holding onto it, I took another step, and my free hand encountered metal shelving. At chest height was something about a yard long and moderately heavy. I picked up the thing, whatever it was, and it swung apart as I retreated through the doorway.

Outside there was enough light for me to see what I carried: a shovel and a set of pruning shears that had fallen open. Clutching them awkwardly against me, too pressed for time to find a better grip, I ran back toward the house, tightening my hold on the sheers as the shovel slipped away from me and fell on the ground. I didn't see any movement by the fence, but it was too dark to tell whether I was still alone in the yard.

On the back of the house was a small porch, the concrete steps leading up to it flanked by large, leafy bushes. Closing the pruning shears, one hand gripping each handle, I crouched on the steps between the bushes.

I can't describe the sound that alerted me to the presence of someone else in the yard. I'm not sure it was a sound. I was alone, and then I wasn't, and someone was moving across the yard, a shadow coming from the side of the house opposite the driveway. The shadow passed me, and I rose as silently as I could, my heart hammering in my chest, and took a step out onto the grass. The shadow moved crablike toward the tool shed, and I took another step, bringing the pruning shears up to my shoulder so that I was holding them like a baseball bat.

The man spun toward me, his left arm rising so that his elbow partially protected his face, but I wasn't aiming for his face. I swung, and the shears thudded against his side, catching him over one of his kidneys. He cried out, staggering, arms flailing and the pistol flying from his hand. I hit him again, this time over the ribs, and he crumpled onto the grass. I let the pruning shears drop to the ground, my face twisting in a savage, grit-teethed grin as I stepped close to kick him in the head with the ball of my sneakered foot.

Arms circled me from behind, pinning my arms against my sides, and I gasped in surprise.

"All right, ma'am. Easy does it now," said the voice in my ear. Warm, oniony breath was on the nape of my neck, and I felt black despair. For an instant, a fraction of a second, my body relaxed as I submitted to my fate, to the man, bigger than I was and stronger, who had me in his grip.

"No!" I shouted and stamped both feet once, twice. The arms about me loosened, allowing me to twist in the grip that held me so that I was looking down into the round face of young man several inches shorter than I was. His eyes were in shadow, his mouth open. I drove my forehead down into his upturned face, and he released me and staggered back, tripping on the pruning sheers I'd dropped and sprawling backwards. The back of his head smacked into one of the concrete steps.

I turned away. The other man, the man I had felled with the pruning shears, was still on the ground, legs beginning to thrash as he struggled to get up, but I stepped on his head on my way to his gun, which lay dark against the grass beyond him. I picked it up, peripherally aware of its clumsiness in my hand, the weight of the slotted cylinder that was screwed onto the end of the barrel.

The gate to the driveway rattled, and a shadow appeared at the top of the fence. Someone was on the woodpile I myself had climbed. A third man. Without even considering the consequences, I pointed the gun at the middle of the fence below the shadow, and I pulled the trigger.

The pistol emitted a hard cough, jerking in my hand as one of the fence's vertical pickets snapped and splintered. There was a curse, inarticulate and disbelieving, and the shadow disappeared.

I ran limping to the back fence, to the gate just past the little tool shed, but I'd forgotten the padlock. I turned, eyes darting to the windows of the house, still dark, then scanning the circling fence, looking for a way of escape. I could feel my pulse in my neck and in the palms of my hands.

The shovel in the middle of the yard. I ran for it, bent to pick it up. The two men were still down, one twitching, the other lying face-up, the back of his head on the concrete step, his smile beatific.

I closed my mind against the implications of that glassy-eyed expression as I propped the shovel against one wall of the tool shed. The edge of the sloping roof was at roughly the height of my chin. Sweat ran down into my eyes, stinging them. I wiped it away as I placed the sole of my sneaker on the shovel's handle at about the middle and, using the shovel as a step, propelled myself up onto the roof.

The asphalt shingles tore at my elbows and knees as I clung to it, scrambling upward the half-dozen feet toward the crest, still clutching the pistol, using my free hand for balance. I stood for a moment, gasping, my heaving lungs no longer able to cope with my body's oxygen needs, and something whined by me.

Turning my head, I saw the shape of a man at the far side of the house. I pointed the pistol and fired, the pistol jerking in my hand as the man dove for cover.

From the roof at the back of the shed, I could look down into the alley beyond the privacy fence. An open trash container was directly below me, its open lid balanced against the fence. It was one of the large plastic containers supplied by the city, and it appeared to be about half-full of weeds and hedge trimmings.

Another whine, and something stung my cheek as I stepped off the roof, bringing my legs together so that I dropped cleanly into the trash container, my legs buckling and my back and my knees jamming against opposite walls. The container rocked with the force of my fall, nearly going over, and the lid closed with a bang above my head.

Chapter 6

I could run no further, but for the moment at least, I was hidden. Time passed and I heard nothing, no one at the locked gate, no one in the alley. That was good and bad. The end of a branch was jabbed into one of my legs, and the air in the container was hot and stale. The close quarters and the sudden cessation of movement opened up my pores, and sweat poured out of me.

Breathing through my mouth, I shifted my position, keeping the gun up, the cooling barrel against my cheek. Then I froze. Voices, coming closer.

"We've lost her. They won't be happy about that."

"We can go back to her house. She has to return there sometime."

"Maybe."

"Maybe she is in there."

My hand tightened on the grip of the gun so hard that it began to cramp.

"If she made it into the house…"

A short laugh. "He's in no condition to help her."

No response. Who was in no condition to help

me? My eyes cut to the gun in my numb fingers. The guy I'd hit with the pruning shears had been carrying this. The other one? The guy I'd head-butted onto the steps? *All right, ma'am, easy does it.* Was he the man who lived here? Had he grabbed me only because he'd just seen me whack a man with his pruning shears?

I strained my ears to hear more, but my tormentors had fallen silent. There were a lot more things I would like them to stand there and discuss, but they didn't oblige me. Time passed, and I continued breathing in short, shallow breaths in the stifling air of the garbage container.

When I heard the crunch of tires on gravel, I'd already endured all I could take. Grasping the pistol with both hands, I lurched from my crouch, driving up the cupped lid of the trash container with the top of my head. I thrust the gun at the windshield of the Ford sedan that was rolling toward me, and it jerked to a stop. The light of the security lamps overhead revealed an old man with a seamed face and rimless glasses, both hands on the wheel, and beside him a stocky woman clutching a purse against her chest. Her eyes were wide, her mouth a tiny "o." I tried a smile and a wave to reassure them, as if a girl with a gun popping out of a trash container could ever be reassuring, but the movement only upset the container, and it went over with a thump that threw me onto the gravel in the path of their headlights.

There was a jolt of gears, and the engine whined as the headlights receded, the light bouncing from fence to fence as the Ford reversed down the alley. They were gone; they would be calling the police, but I didn't care. The breeze, faint as it was, felt so fresh and cool that it might have been blowing out of a window-unit.

I lay there for perhaps a minute, then I picked up the pistol I'd dropped and climbed awkwardly to my feet. After my cramped immobility, I was almost too stiff to move.

When I got to the end of the alley, limping less as my muscles warmed, I lowered the pistol to hold it discreetly against my leg. I wanted nothing so much as to get home, but at the moment I was afraid of my little house on Beechnut. I turned toward John Parker's apartment complex, a little less than two miles away. He had company, but Wendy Walters was just going to have to pardon the interruption. By my calculations I owed her a face full of spit.

It was a bit more than half-an-hour later when I trudged up the steps to John's apartment door, stood on the bare concrete, and rang the doorbell. A two-note chime sounded inside the apartment, but there were no answering footsteps. I waited a moment, then rang the bell again. After another moment I raised my fist to pound on the door.

"Robin?"

I spun, falling back against the door at the sound of the voice coming up from behind me. It was John. His hair was tousled, but he was wearing jeans, an orange T-shirt, and sandals.

"What are you doing here?" He was already on the steps, taking them two at a time. "Are you all right?"

He looked so good to me right then that it was hard to focus on his small failings, like his being a low-down cheat and a miserable excuse for a human being.

"Where have you been?" I asked. My voice grated unnaturally, and he stopped three steps short of the top.

"Is that a gun?"

I raised my hand to look at it. "I guess it is."

"Did something happen?"

I shook my head at him as he climbed the remaining steps to reach me. He didn't touch me.

"You smell funny," he said.

"I've been hiding in a garbage bin, and I need to use your phone."

"What happened?"

"Are you going to unlock your door, or are we just going to stand here?"

He moved past me, keys in hand. As he pushed the door open, I brushed past him into the apartment. "So are you going to tell me what happened or not?" he asked.

"Not, I think."

In the living room I put the gun on the table at the end of the sofa and picked up the phone. I punched 9-1-1, and, as I put the phone to my ear, my eyes went to the sofa itself, so recently occupied by John and Wendy.

"You're a pig, John Parker," I said, listening to the ring of the handset.

"What's gotten into you?"

"Nine-one-one," the voice on the phone said.

I took a breath as I thought how to reduce my recent experience to a sentence or two.

"Hello?"

"I'm here. I'm calling because I was assaulted tonight on the street outside my home."

46

"That's at the Cedar Creek Apartments? Who is this?"

"Cedar Creek is where I'm calling from. My name is Robin Starling." I gave them my address and a brief sketch of what had happened. John's face, I noticed, had gone still. I turned away from it.

"You never saw these men before?" the dispatcher asked.

"No, never. They were waiting for me on the street. I'm afraid they may have been in my house, though." I wet my dry lips. "I'm afraid they may be there now."

"We'll send a car by to check it out."

"I was hoping you could send someone here to take me home. Maybe they could go in with me so I could get my wallet and some I.D. and go to a hotel."

"I think we can do that."

When I had hung up, John was still looking at me. "I'll take you home, if you want to go," he said.

"You don't want to mess with these guys."

John's eyes went to the gun on the end table.

"This is terrible," he said.

"Isn't it, though." I dropped onto his sofa, for the moment heedless of the grass clippings and whatever else might be clinging to my clothes and skin.

"Were they trying to…" He trailed off, and I shook my head, my eyes resting reflectively on his face.

"No, I don't think so," I said. "You never answered my question."

"What question?"

"The one about where you've been."

There was a silence.

"Let me help you out," I said. "Your parking space was empty, so you've been someplace in your car."

I paused, but the silence just settled deeper.

"You could have been visiting your girlfriend," I said, "except that I'm your girlfriend and I wasn't home."

"I could have run to the store for Advil," he said.

I smiled. "Yes, you could have. You had a headache and couldn't sleep, so you made a run to Walgreens. I think maybe I could buy that—except that you didn't have anything in your hands when you got back. Are you keeping Advil in your glovebox now?"

"What, do you want to go down and look in my glove box?"

"I might. Or we could check your bathroom cabinet. I'm pretty sure I remember a bottle of Advil that was still half full."

"What are you trying to prove? What does it matter where I was?"

I raised my shoulders and dropped them. "You tell me."

There was a pause. "After what's happened to you, I guess you're entitled to be upset," he said.

I exhaled, loudly. "You don't know the half of it," I said. I stood abruptly. "They're sending a cruiser. I'll wait outside."

He raised his arms, hands open toward me, and I suddenly found myself badly in need of a hug. I stepped toward him, and, as his arms went around me, put my head on his shoulder and hugged him back, fiercely. My eyes, though they were squeezed shut, began to leak.

"This isn't a good idea," I said, thickly.

"What isn't a good idea?"

Crap. I'd said it out loud. I pulled back. "Two women in one night are bound to overtax you," I said. "I'll see you tomorrow." I kissed his cheek, then skipped backward and slipped out the door.

I didn't look back until I got to the bottom of the stairs. He was there in the doorway, his shadowed face expressionless. I had no idea what he was thinking, or whether he was thinking anything at all.

Chapter 7

Women provide some of the more egregious examples of sexism. I had called for a cop, and they sent me a cop. But, when the cruiser pulled up against the curb, the cop who got out was a short dumpy woman in an ill-fitting uniform, her gun belt weighed down with a revolver, a nightstick, and assorted paraphernalia. Both uniform and gun belt looked designed for a taller, leaner, more powerfully built person—for a man in fact. She introduced herself as Officer Riley, a name that fit her as poorly as the uniform.

"I'm Robin Starling," I said, extending my hand. Some people have two first names (Jesse James, for example). Some have two last names (Jefferson Davis). Me, I have two bird names; I don't know why. Both my parents seemed genuinely startled when, as a teenager, I pointed it out to them. That was the year before Dad left.

"I understand you'd like me to follow you home," Officer Riley said. Her nasal intonation was the one thing that fit her perfectly.

"I don't have a car here. I guess I was hoping I could ride with you."

"Okey dokey."

I tried not to cringe as I followed her around the patrol car. *Okey dokey?* Clint Eastwood wouldn't have said okey dokey. Daniel Craig wouldn't say okey dokey. She opened the passenger door for me, and, as I bent to get in, I tugged the revolver from the waistband at the small of my back so it wouldn't stick into me when I sat down. Officer Riley's hand closed on my wrist. Her grip-strength was surprising, but, in any case, I didn't try to pull away.

"What's that?" she said.

I figured she knew it was a gun. "I took it from one of the guys who was chasing me."

With her free hand, she flapped open a handkerchief. She used it to take the pistol from me, then went around to the back of the car to pop the trunk.

When she got back in the cruiser, she didn't have the gun with her. "It's been fired," she said matter-of-factly.

"Yes."

"You do the firing?"

"Some of it. I think it's been fired more than once."

"Unh huh." She put the car in gear. "Why don't you tell me about it?"

"I already told the dispatcher."

"I haven't seen the transcript. Tell me."

I told the story, and she listened. When I was done, she said, "Let's go back to when you hit the man with the pruning shears."

"He had a gun," I said defensively.

"The gun I took from you just now. Yes, I got that. You hit the man with the pruning shears, and just as he went down, another man grabbed you from behind."

"Yes. I broke away from him, and he fell back and hit his head on the back steps." Okay, so I'd driven my forehead down into his unprotected face. I didn't see any reason to clutter the story with a lot of irrelevant minutia.

"And this was the man who approached you initially," Riley said.

"I thought so."

"You don't think so now?"

"He may have been too short—and after he went down, another man showed up at the fence. I don't know where he came from. I'd been running until I was about to collapse, and suddenly they were all around me."

"One thing you seem a little unclear on is where this final confrontation took place."

"Several blocks from my house. I'm pretty sure I could find it again."

"No need. It was 3490 Darby Drive," Riley said.

"Huh?"

"We had a call from the householder. He heard a commotion in his backyard, saw movement, went out just in time to see a tall young woman clobber someone with what he took to be a baseball bat but turned out to be—"

"Pruning shears." I felt sick, seeing the image of his fixed gaze staring up into the night sky. "Was he hurt?"

"He declined an ambulance."

I thought that was a bad call on his part. We

52

turned onto my street, which was illuminated by a street light every block or so. It was now close to midnight. There were no cars on the street, and the houses were all dark—all except mine. The curtains in my front window glowed with the lights of the living room.

"See anything unusual?" Riley asked me as we pulled up against the curb in front of my house.

"No."

"You left the lights on then?"

I tried to think back to the time when I passed the house at the end of my run. It had been dark by then. Had the lights been on? I couldn't remember. "I don't know," I said. "Probably. It was daylight when I left the house."

"Let's go."

We got out together. Riley stopped at the end of my sidewalk. "Where was this car exactly?"

"Right there." I pointed across the street. "Directly across from the sidewalk."

She crossed the street, and I crossed with her, my eyes scanning for evidence: traces of condensation that had dripped from the car's air conditioner, the cigarette butt I had seen one of them toss away— anything. I didn't even see the cigarette butt.

Officer Riley turned back toward the house, her hand going to rest on the butt of her gun. "Let's go in."

My front door was closed and locked, just as it should be. No scars on the wood or on the lock itself suggested that anyone without a key had tried to get in. I slipped the string with my house key over my head and unlocked the door. My living room was in the same state as I had left it.

I glanced at Riley, wondering if my story was beginning to seem as fantastic to her as it was to me. If so, she gave no sign. Together we walked through the house, checking the windows as well as the condition of each room.

"Everything's normal," I said. The stress of anticlimax was apparent in the unsteadiness of my voice. I cleared my throat. "I don't guess they've been inside."

"No."

"I guess it ought to make me feel better."

"Doesn't it?"

"They wanted something from me, and I don't have any idea what it is."

"Want me to wait while you pack a bag?"

I shook my head. "I'll be all right."

"You sure?"

I wasn't, not by a long shot, but I nodded and said, "I'll lock the door behind you."

She walked out, moving with the rolling gait that had added to my first, false impression of her. I locked the door and turned, my back against it. All the lights in the house were still on after our brief walk-through, and I couldn't see myself turning any of them off. Outside, the door of the police cruiser slammed, the sound followed a moment later by the roar of the engine. The skin on my bare arms broke out in gooseflesh.

"Oh, heck," I said, wishing I had accepted her offer to wait. Moving quickly, I got a silk dress from my bedroom closet, a clean bra and panties from the dresser, and my travel case from the bathroom. On my way out to the garage, I snatched up my purse from the recliner in the living room.

The purse had evidently been lying open. My keys fell out of it and onto the floor along with my ChapStick, my Listerine strips, and a makeup compact. I stopped, a feeling of horror creeping over me as I looked down into my open purse. Maybe…Maybe someone had been in the house after all, and whoever it was had gone through my purse.

Though my wallet was still there in the purse. That was puzzling. I set down the travel case to get it out and found my cash and credit cards still inside. I closed the wallet thoughtfully, then put the stuff that had fallen out back into the purse. I picked up my travel case and change of clothes again, and continued on out to the garage. I tossed everything into the passenger seat of my Beetle and swung down into it.

I'd forgotten my briefcase, I realized.

The doorbell rang as I reentered the house, and, if the ceiling had been any lower, I think I would have hit my head on it. Then a key rasped in the lock, and my adrenal gland dumped the rest of its contents into my bloodstream. I hotfooted it toward the front door, casting about for something to use for a weapon, silently cursing Riley for taking the pistol.

I grabbed up a table lamp with a heavy brass base, yanking the plug from the wall by the cord. The shade made it awkward, but I didn't have time to look for anything else. The front door was swinging inward, and I stepped behind it with the upside-down lamp gripped firmly in both hands.

The man who entered was wearing an orange T-shirt and faded jeans. I exhaled in noisy relief, and John Parker jumped and spun.

"Holy crap! You scared the bejeebers out of me," he said.

It was one of the things I'd always liked about John. Most men would have said something a good deal stronger than bejeebers. "You didn't do my nerves any good either," I pointed out as I put the lamp back on its table. "What are you doing here?"

"I came to help."

"Seems a bit late for that. What did you have in mind?"

"I don't know. Serve and protect? I saw the cop drive off."

"She didn't see you lurking around out there?" My respect and admiration for Riley dipped a bit. Lurking men in automobiles were what this was about, after all.

"She?" John asked.

"The cop. Women can be cops."

"I was just turning the corner as she pulled away."

"I was about to take off myself."

"Where to? You want to come to my place?"

"I was thinking of a hotel."

"I'll go with you."

"I think your prostate's had enough stimulation for one evening, don't you?"

"You keep saying that," he said, though I could have sworn it was the first time I'd mentioned his prostate. "I don't know what you're talking about."

"I'm talking about a leggy brunette named Wendy Walters."

"Wendy..." He processed the new data quickly, as one might expect a trial lawyer to do. "She came out on the balcony, didn't she? You saw her."

"And her clothing wasn't arranged so that it covered her all that well," I said.

He took a breath. "I'm sorry, Robin. I was actually

trying to help."

My eyebrows went up.

"She called me about three o'clock, said she tried to get you, but you weren't in your office."

I thought back. Probably in the employee lounge with Cynthia and Pete Larsen.

"She left work early—something about somebody going through her desk and her briefcase or something. Anyway, it got unpleasant, and she wanted to talk to you."

"Okay."

"She lives in Shockoe Bottom, you know. Her commute home took her right by the office."

"And so you went down to the street, and she picked you up."

He took a breath and let it out. "She wanted someone to go home with her to check out the place—you know, like you and the cop. That's what we did, anyway. We went down to her place on Main Street. The door was locked. She opened it on some stairs, and then she just stood there, looking up. Well, it was a bit much. 'Can we get on with this?' I said. 'I'm in trial tomorrow. I gotta get back to work.' It's the Gardner case, you know."

I nodded.

"She just looked at me, biting her lip. Then she stepped back outside, closed the door, and locked it up again. She headed back to her car, and I followed, thinking, well, fine, at least this little excursion won't have cost me more than half-an-hour." He stopped.

I said, "So how's that trial prep coming? You ready?"

"Actually, I had a message waiting for me at home. Trial got postponed again."

"How convenient." I stood looking at him, and evidently the scrutiny made him uncomfortable.

"It was weird, really," he said. "She kept looking at me as she drove, sizing me up or something."

"And she had those long legs underneath the steering wheel," I prompted.

"Well, yeah. I let her take us to my place. You know the rest."

"Ah. The trials and tribulations of being irresistible to women."

His eyes were distant, as if he were replaying some scene or other. Finally, he said, "Look, I know she's your friend and all, but that Wendy is one weird chick."

"But not so weird that it put you off."

"I, uh." He smiled weakly. "You can put up with a lot of weirdness from a naked woman."

If I'd still been holding the table lamp, I would have brained him with it, but I'd already plugged it back in. "Why don't you just get the hell out of here?" I said instead. "Just get the hell out." I brushed past him, heading for the den. In addition to being exhausted generally, I was suddenly exhausted with John Parker.

"What?" he called after me. "I didn't tell you anything you didn't already know. What is it?"

"I'm not naked. What do you care?" I couldn't find my briefcase. It hadn't been by the recliner where I tossed my purse. It wasn't at the end of the counter in the kitchen. I thought I'd try my bedroom, but I ran into John in the kitchen doorway.

"Oh, forget it," I said. "I can go for a day without a briefcase."

"Can I help?"

"Yes. You can lock the front door behind you on your way out."

"You're really going to a hotel? It doesn't look like anyone's been in here."

"I don't care what it looks like. I'm going to get a good night's sleep."

"I could stay here with you," he said. "Sleep on the couch."

"You can sleep on the couch if you want to. I won't be here. I'm leaving."

And I did. He was looking after me as the garage door lowered between us, crouching lower and lower to maintain eye contact as long as possible. I made a face and shook my head as I backed into the alley and switched the car into drive. John was a charmer, I'd give him that. Couldn't keep his pecker in his pants to save his life, but he was a charmer.

Chapter 8

My office, when I walked into it the next morning, was a mess—though no more so than normal. On my desk were books, client files, and legal pads covered with scribbled notes, as well as pencils, pens, and highlighters of various colors. On the credenza behind my desk was my computer, screen on, waiting for a user-name and password. No briefcase in evidence, so evidently I hadn't left it here.

I sank into my chair and typed: rstarlin, slamdunk. My desktop came up. I clicked on the Windows Explorer icon, then on the file I'd been working on the day before when Cynthia had appeared in my doorway with her tale of woe. My billable hours begun, I sat back and thought about Wendy Walters, a subject that had occupied me much of the night.

I'd had it coming, I had to give her that. For some, ten years might be long enough to wipe the ledger clean, but I could see how for others it might not. Maybe fifty years wouldn't be enough. If we happened to end up in the same nursing home, Wendy might be wheeling her chair into the lounge intent on seducing whatever eighty-year-old hottie I was sweet on in retaliation for Cody.

I turned my chair to get my purse out of the knee well of my desk, thinking I ought to take a look at the CD she'd given me. It wasn't in my purse. I looked for my briefcase, then remembered it had gone missing. I sat back. This wasn't good.

"Robin?" It was John's voice.

I swiveled and, when I saw him standing awkwardly in the doorway, kicked back and braced a foot against my desk. "John Parker," I said. "As I live and breathe."

"I locked up before I left."

I nodded, my mouth pursed, my eyes dropping to my fuchsia-colored pump. Only a half-inch heel, but it looked good against the dark wood, I thought.

"I looked around for your briefcase some more," John said. "It's not in any of the usual places."

"Did you check my bedroom?"

He nodded.

"I didn't check the bedroom," I said.

"It's not there. What else is missing, anything?"

"Just the briefcase. Maybe a CD out of my purse. It fell open when I picked it up last night."

"A CD? What kind of CD?"

"A Taylor Swift CD."

He looked puzzled. "That's not your kind of music."

"Not as far as you know," I said.

"So what are you thinking? Somebody stole your briefcase and then a Taylor Swift CD out of your purse?"

"I don't know."

He remained in the doorway, looking as if he were

61

about to say something conciliatory, but I wasn't ready to reconcile.

"Heard from Wendy?" I asked. "Or did you and she not part on a good note?"

His flinch was almost imperceptible. "No, actually, we didn't. Things fell apart pretty quickly after you saw her on the balcony. It wasn't thirty minutes later she was driving me back downtown to get my car."

I looked down again at the point of my shoe, nodding unhappily. "Well, she finally got me."

"What do you mean by that? You can't be thinking she came onto me just because you and I are together."

"Maybe."

"Aren't you being a little conceited?"

"One of us is."

He made a face. "You want me to apologize? Is that what this is about?"

I shrugged. "What's the point of apologizing? It's not like you could have done any different. If Wendy Walters set out to seduce you, then you were going to be seduced. Smile at you, show a little leg—it'd be like hitting you in the head with a poleax."

He grinned, but it had a defensive look to it. I stayed on offense.

"You know, when I was fifteen, my father ran off with a twenty-two-year-old named Jasmine. Can you believe that? Jasmine."

"I thought your father was a veterinarian."

Talk about your non sequitur. "Veterinarians can't be philanderers?" I said. "Jasmine was his veterinary assistant."

"It's just that, from the stories you told, I thought you had a good relationship with your father."

"I did. Right up until he took off. And I've gotten over that, so don't worry about me. You're just one more chapter in my *Men Are Weasels* field guide."

"I…" He gave up with a shrug and stepped out of the doorway. The walls were transparent, though, so I got to watch him walk away.

My triumph should have felt better than it did, but I had just unloaded a dump truck of emotional baggage on him, which might not have been entirely fair. He hadn't promised to love and honor me until death us did part. He had only obliged me with sex when I'd wanted it. It had felt like love for a lifetime, but of course it wasn't. Somehow it never was.

With a start, I realized that someone else had appeared in my doorway. It was Pete Larsen, the firm's managing partner.

"Hello, Robin."

My foot was still propped on the desk, and his gaze cut to my bare leg—or maybe he was just admiring my fuchsia pump.

"Hello, Pete."

"Are you wearing stockings?" he said.

We both looked at my leg. I looked back up at him. "No, Pete, I guess I'm not."

"Stockings make for a more professional image. Especially if you're going to keep your feet on your desk."

Probably that wasn't very professional either. I sighed and put my foot down. I started to tell him that women's hosiery had gone out of fashion a decade ago, maybe two, but I refrained. Maybe Pete's wife wore hose. "It was an oversight," I said.

He nodded, almost to himself, turned, and continued down the hall.

"Crap," I said to myself as I picked up a pen and dragged over a legal pad. Caught once again in an unladylike posture. There were men in the firm who put their feet on their desks all the time—Eric Beezer lay on his desk like a supine Buddha—but I suspected that keeping *my* feet on *my* desk wasn't a good way to make partner.

For a good ten minutes I tried to focus on the work in front of me. Larry Briggs' Homes was paying three hundred dollars an hour for my time, and already I owed them—I glanced at my watch—eek, almost a hundred and fifty bucks. I was going to have to be extraordinarily productive to make it up to them.

But I couldn't concentrate. Wendy had seemed genuinely frightened. On top of that, I had been assaulted, and the CD she'd given me had disappeared. Taken together, it all seemed to suggest something sinister going on.

I snatched up the phone and dialed information. There was a phone book in my desk, but I hadn't used it since my first year as an associate attorney. "Richmond," I said in answer to the usual question. "McCormack Labs."

I got the number and punched it in.

"McCormack Labs," a voice said.

"Wendy Walters, please."

After half-a-dozen rings I got her voice mail. "Wendy, this is Robin," I said. "Call me back." I gave my number and hung up.

I sat staring at the phone.

I picked up the phone and dialed McCormack Labs again. "Is Wendy Walters in the office today?" I asked. "I've already spoken to her voicemail. I just want to know if she's there."

"Moment please."

After several moments, a male voice came on. "Accounting."

"Yes, I'm trying to reach Wendy Walters."

"I'll give you her voicemail."

"Is she out sick, or…"

"She hasn't come in yet. I'm her supervisor. Is it something I can help you with?"

"No. It's personal, not professional." I hung up, thinking too late that his phone might be equipped with Caller ID, just as mine was. If so, Wendy's supervisor knew someone at the Northcutt law firm was calling for her.

I checked my wristwatch. It was nearly ten-thirty. Calling information again, I asked for Wendy Walters. There were a lot of Walters living in Richmond. No Wendy, but there was a W. Walters on Main Street with a street number that should put it in Shockoe Bottom, which was where John had said Wendy lived.

An answering machine picked up on the fourth ring, Wendy's voice repeating her phone number. I hung up without leaving a message.

I looked at my watch. I had to be at a docket call in forty-five minutes, which didn't leave a lot of time for anything else. I glanced at the computer screen, where work for Larry Briggs' Homes was progressing, but not very fast.

Most of my practice involved suing people, but Larry Briggs was a client I had on the defense side of the docket. I stood up. Today, Larry Briggs was going to have to look after himself. I got a file folder out of the big, lateral file cabinet and glanced around for my briefcase to put it in before I realized I no longer had a briefcase. What I did have was a little leather portfolio my mother had given me for Christmas. It was small, just big enough to hold a standard-sized folder, and my folder was legal-sized, so I had to fold up the bottom to make it fit.

I found a parking place on the street next to the courthouse, a bit of good luck that seemed out of keeping with my recent experiences. As I approached the main entrance, I glanced toward the house that Chief Justice John Marshall had lived in. It was next door to the courthouse, and I thought, for the hundredth time, that someday I was going to have to take the tour.

In the courtroom my case was called. I announced ready, and the lawyer for the defense asked for a continuance. The judge, an overweight, jowly guy in his fifties, said, "I can see by the case number that you're entitled," and that was that. The case was continued. It was a simple case that didn't require any more discovery, so there was no reason for a continuance, but the wheels of justice sometimes get ahead of themselves and pause in their grinding for no particular reason.

As I walked back into the late summer heat, I got out my cell phone and tried again to reach Wendy at her office.

"I'll give you her voice mail."

"Wait, I—" But of course it was too late. I'd been transferred even before the receptionist finished speaking. I hung up and tried Wendy's apartment, where I got her answering machine.

"It figures," I said to no one in particular. I beeped my car unlocked and got inside.

Chapter 9

Shockoe Bottom is a valley between downtown Richmond and Church Hill, the city's oldest neighborhood. A hundred years ago, the Bottom was the center of the city's tobacco industry. Flooding has wiped it out a number of times, most recently just a couple of years ago when a tropical storm dropped twelve inches of rain over the James River's watershed. The clubs, restaurants, and shops were just beginning to come back.

Wendy, it turned out, lived in the apartment over a newly renovated bar and grill at the corner of 19th and Main. The entrance to the apartment, a few feet down from the restaurant's, was a wide red door with a large pane of glass in its upper half. The door was, predictably, locked—with a double-keyed deadbolt, I saw, my forehead pressed to the glass. No one could open the door without a key, even from the inside.

I rang the bell and waited, glancing toward the entrance of the restaurant, which didn't seem to be getting much traffic even at the noon-hour. The sound of hammering was coming from somewhere about halfway down the block. I backed away and looked up at the windows, which consisted of large panes of time-rippled glass. For a moment, I thought I saw movement, and I raised my hand in a wave, but nobody waved back.

I went back to the door and rang the bell again, then again backed out into the street to look up at the windows. Nothing this time, not even a hint of movement.

I walked back around the corner of the restaurant to look up at Wendy's apartment from 19th Street. On that side the apartment had a narrow balcony with a wooden balustrade painted the same shade of crimson as the door on Main. It was about fifteen feet above the sidewalk, and there was nothing below it but fifteen feet of blank brick wall.

As I stood looking up, a power saw whined in the distance and a board fell with a muffled clunk. I stepped toward Main Street and looked down the block. A pickup loaded with boards and tools stood on the street about a half-block down. An extension ladder was strapped to a black metal frame that rose above the pickup's bed.

I walked down. The door of the shop nearest the pickup was propped open. Inside were two men about my age. They were cutting boards, one standing at either end of a stack of them propped on a pair of sawhorses. Both wore shorts and work boots. One wore a T-shirt with Curt Colbain's picture on the front. The one with the Skil saw was shirtless, exposing a tattoo of Porky Pig on one shoulder and a tattoo of a Chinese dragon on the other. The saw whined briefly as they looked at me, their eyes going first to my face, then dropping to check out the rest of me. Ordinarily, this automatic physical assessment by those of the male persuasion irritates the crap out of me, but ordinarily I don't want something.

I smiled, and the guy with the saw smiled back reflexively. He had too much in the way of sideburns for my taste, but the tattoos didn't bother me, and he was built like a Greek statue come to life. "Hi," I said.

"Hi," said the guy in the shirt. Apollo waved his fingers at me.

"I seem to have locked myself out of my apartment." I blinked at them, which is about as close as I can come to an eye-flutter. "It would be really helpful if I could borrow your ladder," I said.

For a moment they just looked at me. Then the guy in the shirt straightened, and Apollo put down his saw. "Sure." "Okay."

"Great," I said.

There was a little awkwardness in the doorway, since I was standing in it. They hesitated, unsure how to get past without rubbing their sweaty, sawdust-speckled bodies against me. Since my dress was silk, which stains like nobody's business, I stepped aside. Physical contact with sweaty, well-built men would have to wait for a more auspicious occasion.

They had the ladder off the truck in about ten seconds, and I was leading them down the sidewalk and around the corner. I pointed to the balcony, and they put the end of the ladder on the sidewalk and pulled on a rope to raise the ladder to the necessary height. They leaned it against the wall next to the balcony.

"Thanks," I said, a hand on a rung of the ladder. "I really appreciate this."

"Don't you want one of us to...?"

"No, this is fine."

I started up, and it evidently took two of them to steady the ladder, because they each stood with a hand on it, looking up as I climbed. My biggest regret was that I couldn't sell popcorn.

When I got to the top and reached out for the top of the balcony railing, I discovered a problem. My dress, though not all that long, was too tight to allow me to keep one foot on the ladder and reach the edge of the balcony with my other foot. I looked down. My two helpers were looking up at me.

"Are you all right?" one said.

"Just stuck." I only saw one way to do this, and it wasn't particularly modest. My dress, fortunately, wasn't the only thing that was new. My underwear was new, too—peach colored panties with a lacy top. They didn't match my fuchsia pumps, of course, but last night when I was grabbing things to take to the hotel, I hadn't seen the need to color coordinate. I looked down again to where the guys were smiling encouragement.

Amateur night on a ladder in Shockoe Bottom. I hiked my dress up around my hips and took a big step sideways, sliding the toe of my pump beneath the rail of the balcony and grabbing the top of the balustrade with one hand. I brought my other hand and my other foot across so that I was standing, legs together, on the outside of the balcony railing, gripping the top of it with both hands. Looking at my reflection in the two windows that faced onto the porch, I could see my legs all the way to my waist. Great.

I swung one leg over the railing, then the other, and allowed my dress to fall back into place, a little wrinkled, but otherwise undamaged—which was a relief, because this was only the second or third time

I'd worn it. I rested my forearms on the rail to look over. The two men were looking up at me, and they seemed at little dazed, as if they'd just been slapped in the face with a large wet tuna.

"Thanks, guys. You're life-savers," I said.

"Oh, ah, you're welcome. What's your name?"

I hesitated, unsure whether to give them my name, Wendy's name, or to make one up completely. "Robin," I said. "Robin Starling."

The name of the guy without the shirt was Steve. "And this is Dustin," Steve said.

Dustin nodded and smiled at me.

"Thanks, Steve. Dustin." I gave them my best smile, then stood watching as they lowered the ladder and disappeared with it around the corner.

The solid wood door at the end of the narrow porch turned out to be locked, so I turned to look at the windows. One of them was closed and latched, but the other stood open a full inch, which struck me as being neither very security-conscious nor energy efficient. There were no screens.

I bent and poked at the curtain that blocked my view of the interior. "Hey, Wendy!" I called through the gap. "It's Robin Starling."

There was no answer. Poking at the curtain with my finger showed me no more than an uncarpeted wood floor and the edge of a bed. I hooked my fingers under the frame of the sash and tugged upward, but it was stuck. I stepped out of my shoes, braced my feet in a wide stance, and drove upward against the top of the frame with the heels of my hands. Nothing budged.

I put my face against the window, trying to see whether the lower sash had been nailed in place, but I couldn't tell. Probably the wood had swollen over time, or else someone had painted the window in place.

Bracing myself again, I took a breath and pushed up on the sash with everything I had, a deep guttural sound forcing its way through my throat. A second passed as I strained upward. Two seconds. Three.

I dropped my hands and gasped for air.

"Door locked up there, too?" It was Dustin, coming to check up on me.

"Yeah. I thought I could go in through the window, but it's stuck tight. I may have to get you to bring back that ladder."

"Want me to come up and try? We've got a couple of pinch bars. We can have that thing open in no time."

He had a nice face, I thought. "Let me try one more thing first," I said. I'd tried raising the lower sash, but hadn't tried lowering the top. I turned back to the window and hung my fingers on the crosspiece of the upper sash. I sagged against the window, letting it take as much of my weight as my fingertips would support. It gave slightly, or I thought it did.

"Is it coming?" Dustin called.

I redoubled my effort, sagging against the window, easing up, sagging, easing up.

"You getting it?"

"I...think...so."

The window gave suddenly, dropping all the way to the bottom. The glass panes rattled, but didn't break, which was something.

"I got it," I called down to Dustin.

He nodded encouragement from the street, having stepped back far enough to keep me in view.

"I'm going in now," I said. "Thanks."

"Oh, you're welcome." He continued to stand there, grinning up at me in the strong sunlight.

The sill of the window was about six inches above the floor of the balcony. I stepped up on it and ducked my head to get it in the window, using my free hand to push at the curtain. The sashes were about three feet high, so there was no question of stepping through. I was going to have to go through on my belly.

I stepped down and considered my new dress, which I'd already sweated through in places. At the moment it was salvageable, but this was going to finish it, stretching and ripping it in any number of ways.

I hesitated, looking back over the rail at Dustin. "I'm going to have to…" I took a breath. "Oh, heck with it." I reached behind my neck to unfasten the clasp at the top of my dress and get the zipper started, then pushed the dress off one shoulder and then the other. The zipper slid a bit more, and the dress fell to the floor and puddled around my feet. I stepped out of it.

I glanced down at Dustin, but he seemed to have petrified on me. "Don't want to ruin my dress," I called by way of explanation. I picked up the dress and tossed it through the open window. I was, unfortunately, wearing a beige bra with my peach panties, and it was a plain, serviceable bra without a trace of lace, but what can you do?

Bending to get my shoes, I tossed one and then the other through the window after my dress.

"Bye now," I called to Dustin.

He raised a hand in a vague sort of wave. I stepped

onto the sill and put my head and shoulders through the window, trying not to think of the rear view I was giving Dustin and any passing traffic. Bracing my hands on the tops of the two window sashes, I pushed up into the hanging curtain with my back arched and my feet pressing against the inner edge of the window frame for balance. This brought my hips up to rest on the top of the sashes. From there I rolled into the apartment, the heels of my bare feet catching for a moment on the frame of the window, then catching in the curtains. Both curtains and curtain rod came with me as I completed an inelegant somersault and landed on my butt.

I was inside, sitting on the uncarpeted floor in what looked like Wendy's bedroom. Beside me was a double bed on an old-fashioned iron frame, unmade, with a rumpled quilt near the foot. There was a small throw rug beside the bed; I'd missed it by inches.

Disentangling my feet from the fallen curtain, I got up, moving gingerly from having just been hit in the fanny by a hardwood floor. I shook out my dress and put it on, looking about me. A wardrobe stood open against the wall opposite the bed. As with many of these old apartments, there was no closet.

I bent to retrieve my shoes and walked out of the bedroom into a short hall. The bathroom that opened off it was so small it looked like you'd have to stand in the bathtub to close the door. Holding one shoe in each hand, I walked past the bathroom, passing over a vent blowing cold air that felt good on my bare legs. At the end of the hall was the living room, and that was where my investigation ended. Wendy was sprawled on a long sofa upholstered in a faded floral pattern, and she was naked but for a bra and panties.

I approached her body with almost a reverent awe. There was cord around her neck that looked like a piece of clothesline. Her eyes were fixed and staring, and her skin looked strangely pale beneath her tan. I knelt beside her, touching a hand to her bare stomach. She was probably room temperature, more or less, but for a human being she was cold—shockingly so.

The side of her body, of her chest and hips, was two toned, pale on top and a bluish tint closer to the couch. I knew the cause from an autopsy film I'd seen in law school. The blood was settling, responding to the force of gravity rather than that of a beating heart. I couldn't remember how long it took for that to become noticeable, but she'd been dead awhile.

I glanced at my watch—12:15. At the upper limit, she'd been dead no more than fifteen hours, because I'd seen her alive fifteen hours ago, alive and standing on a balcony with one John Parker. At the thought, goose bumps broke out all over my body, and my heart kicked it up a notch. About thirteen hours ago John had just been getting home, having come from delivering Wendy to her apartment. Looking down at Wendy's body, I found it all too easy to believe that thirteen hours ago Wendy had been dead.

I walked back through the apartment in a daze, looking at everything, but not really seeing any of it. I felt somehow as if someone else were there, lurking just outside my field of vision.

Of course, someone was there, and I went back to the living room and sat by her. Wendy's clothes were lying carelessly on the floor at the end of the couch, the same blouse and skirt she had worn to my office. I didn't see her shoes.

I took Wendy's cold fingers loosely between my thumb and forefinger, as my attention returned to the body that looked so much like Wendy Walters and at the same time looked nothing like her. "I'm sorry, Wendy," I said, and for a moment had the feeling she was in the room with me—she herself, and not just her corpse.

I shook my head. My thoughts were crazy, possibly because they were shying from their proper subject, which was the possibility that John Parker had killed Wendy Walters. He had no motive, at least none that I knew of. It was possible that something had gone wrong during some kind of sex game, but it didn't strike me as terribly probable. I'd dated the guy for months, and he'd never tried to put a clothesline around my neck.

On the other hand, she was in her underwear. With John that made a certain amount of sense, but if someone else had come to the apartment door after he had gone, she surely wouldn't have greeted him dressed like that. Or her.

I got up. Someone had killed Wendy. I didn't know who, and I didn't have the resources to find out. It was time to call somebody.

My cell was in my purse, which I had left in the car, but I had seen a phone in her bedroom on the nightstand. As I headed for it, I wondered cowardly if I could slip out of the apartment and give the police an anonymous call from the nearest payphone. No, I had no choice but to face the music. I had been seen entering the apartment, seen in what had to be memorable circumstances. I had also given Steve and Dustin my name, too busy trolling for my next date to exercise even a modicum of caution.

I picked up the cordless telephone and dialed. "Nine-one-one."

I took a breath. "My name is Robin Starling," I said. "I'm afraid I have to report a murder."

Chapter 10

The police were on their way. I slipped into my pumps and sat down in the bedroom to wait. Several minutes ticked by before it occurred to me that I had no way to open the door for the police when they got there. The deadbolt on the door at the bottom of the stairs required a key.

I checked the nightstand for a spare, opening the drawer with my knuckles to avoid leaving prints that might be awkward to explain. There was a lot of stuff in there, from antacids to body lotion, but no key. I shut the drawer. In the kitchen, I checked the walls for a key hanging from a nail or a hook, likewise without success. I went back through the living room to the main door, which opened on the stairway leading down to the street. No spare key hanging on either side of it, though there was a four-penny nail in the wall where Wendy could have hung one.

It was then that I remembered her purse, sitting on a chair in the living room across from the couch. I didn't need a spare key if Wendy's own set was there in her purse. I went to check and came up with a key chain with a silver basketball on the end of it and six keys. I blinked, suddenly fighting back tears. I had a key chain like Wendy's somewhere. Everyone on the team had gotten one when we won the game that took us to the Final Four. I stood there looking at it, then looked again at Wendy.

"I'm sorry about Cody," I said, for the first time. "I'm so sorry."

She didn't answer. What I wanted was forgiveness, but it was too late to get it from Wendy Walters. I looked up at the ceiling. "I'm sorry about all of them," I said to God or to no one in particular. A collage of images swirled through my mind, images of boys and men, Cody and John Parker and others, each the subject of runaway passions and self-indulgence—or so it suddenly seemed to me.

I sat abruptly on the end of the sofa by Wendy's feet, tears streaming down my face, but my repentance brought no feeling of peace or forgiveness. Then a banging on the door at the foot of the stairs brought me to my senses. Whether I was having a spiritual breakthrough or an emotional breakdown, there was no time for it now. I dried my face with the heels of my hands and went down to meet the police.

"Hi," I said in a stopped-up voice. "I'm Robin Starling." I turned and led four of them up the stairs, two in uniforms and two wearing ties and short-sleeve dress shirts.

They looked at the body. I sat in a chair at the kitchen table and watched. After several minutes, one of the men wearing a tie came over and pulled out a chair next to me. He had curly hair shot with gray and a mustache that extended down too far on either side of his mouth.

"My name's Jordan," he said as he sat down.

"Robin Starling."

He nodded. "Do you think you can tell me about it?"

"I think so."

"You discovered the body?"

"A few minutes ago." I checked my watch. "Maybe twenty."

"Do you know who she is?"

"Wendy Walters. She's an accountant at McCormack Labs."

"Did you touch anything?"

"Some things in the bedroom. I got in through the window." Unexpectedly, a convulsive sort of sob burst from me. My chest heaved, and I stopped talking until I could control it. "I touched her," I said finally. "On the stomach." I took a breath. "She was cold."

"How did you know to break into the apartment? Did you know she was dead?"

"No. I had no idea."

He smiled faintly. "You in the habit of breaking into other people's apartments?"

I shook my head. "She came to see me yesterday. I tried to reach her at work and they told me she hadn't come in. She didn't answer her home phone. I didn't know her cell."

"How long have you known her?"

"Twelve years. A little more."

He nodded, then got up and left me. Some more people had shown up, and they were clustered around the body. Every few seconds, someone would shift his position, and I'd get another glimpse of bare flesh. I tried not to look.

Jordan came back. "It's a long way to the ground," he said. "How did you get up onto that balcony?"

"I borrowed a ladder from some workmen a couple of doors down."

"It was you that tore the curtains loose?"

I nodded. "Uh huh."

"And you found her there on the sofa, just like she is now."

I nodded again, knowing there was no danger anyone would think I had moved the body. The settled blood was persuasive testimony that no one had moved her recently.

A young woman with her hair in a ponytail was in the living room now, taking pictures of everything.

"Where do you work?" Jordan asked me.

"Northcutt, Hambrick and Larsen. It's a law firm."

"And you're...?"

"A lawyer." I glanced at him. To judge by my experience with traffic cops, this was equivalent to saying I liked to torture small animals, but if Jordan's expression tightened at all, I couldn't tell it. He continued to sit sprawled in the chair beside me, just a friendly guy making conversation. He was probably fifty, but until you looked at him closely enough to see the network of fine wrinkles around his eyes you wouldn't know it.

I took a breath. "Like I said, Wendy's an accountant at McCormack Labs. Yesterday she told me she'd discovered some accounting irregularities, and she didn't know what to do about it. She said she'd found a second set of books."

Jordan thought about it. "Did she have any documentation to support that?"

He talked pretty well for a cop. "I think so," I said.

"I don't know." I took a breath, hesitating to embark on a story that had to sound melodramatic and overwrought. This was the second time in two days I had dialed 9-1-1, though, and I thought I'd better give some account of it.

I told the story, starting at the end of my run with the man who knew my name. As I talked, Jordan's eyebrows climbed his forehead.

"Eventually, I spilled out of the trash container and walked a couple of miles to a friend's house." No need to mention brandishing the gun at an elderly couple. "I called the police from there, and they sent an Officer Riley to take me home and walk through the house with me."

"How long did it take you to discover the missing disc?"

"A while. The first thing I missed was my briefcase. I still haven't found that. And my purse fell open when I picked it up."

"So these people, whoever they were, broke into your home?"

"It looks that way. I don't know."

"And you have no idea who they are?"

"Not unless they have some connection with Wendy."

It bothered me that his eyebrows still hadn't dropped back to where they were supposed to be.

"You don't believe me," I said.

He moved his head. "If it's the truth, you're stuck with it."

"I guess I am."

He fished out a notebook and a pen. "Let me make sure I've got your name right. You said Robin…Sterling?"

"Starling."

"Starling." He wrote it at the top of a blank page in all caps. "Your address?"

My eyes went back to the living room as he began jotting notes. A couple of guys in their early twenties were dusting for prints. For the moment nobody was near Wendy, pale in her bra and panties, ignored.

"What's your last name?" I asked Jordan.

"Jordan." After a moment, he added, "My first name is James. I have two first names."

"Tell me about it."

He looked at me quizzically, but I didn't elaborate, and he didn't pursue it. After several more minutes of scribbling, he got up and went to talk to his partner, a Hispanic man with a flat face. Too lethargic to move, I sat and watched the technicians at work.

Somehow, I had gotten through my entire statement with no mention of my libidinous boyfriend, and I'd done it without ever making a conscious decision to cover for him. John Parker just didn't have anything to do with McCormack's accounting problems or with the two men who had accosted me outside my home. What had happened to Wendy was all wrapped up with that, at least in my mind. John Parker fell under the heading of Boyfriend Problems, which was something else entirely.

It was maybe forty minutes later when James Jordan got back to me. "You all right?" he asked.

I nodded. "I will be."

"We're going to need your fingerprints for purposes of elimination. Do you think you can stop by the station later this afternoon?" He fished a card out of his shirt pocket and gave it to me. "Ask for me."

"Okay."

"You can go now." He smiled. "I know how to find you."

I had to be back in court at three o'clock for a hearing on a motion for summary judgment, and, because I had to go by my office first to pick up the file, I barely made it to the courthouse on time. I walked into the courtroom about ten seconds before my case was called.

I stood up almost as soon as I'd sat down and pushed through the bar along with a man with reddish blond hair who looked about forty.

I represented the plaintiff, so I went first. "It's a suit on a note, Your Honor," I said. "A copy of the note is attached to the complaint. It's authenticated by the required affidavit from the creditor. No question has been raised in the pleadings as to the legitimacy of the debt."

My opponent disagreed. "There's an ambiguity on the face of the instrument, Your Honor. If you'll look at the note, you'll see that there's a question of fact about the interest rate. It's impossible to tell whether the defendant agreed to pay six and three-eighths or six and five-eighths."

The judge was flipping through his file. I opened mine. On the copy of the promissory note attached to the complaint, I saw what he meant. Where it was written out in words, the interest rate was clearly six and five-eighths. Where it was written numerically, the rate was smudged. It could say six and five-eighths, but it was also possible to read it as six and three.

"I see what you mean," the judge said.

I checked the original, hoping the smudge was only on the photocopy, but, no, it was there, too. I stood up. "Your Honor, even if it did say six and three eighths numerically, when the numerals contradict the numbers as written out, the words control."

The judge looked thoughtful, but I'd run into him before and had my doubts. "That's true for a check," he said. "But is it true for a promissory note?"

I didn't know, but thought it had to be. "They're both negotiable instruments."

"It raises a question of fact for the jury," my opponent said.

I said, "It raises a question of law. I can have it briefed for you by tomorrow."

"Even if the wording does control," my opponent said, "my client may have relied on the numerical representation of the interest rate, which raises the question of mistake and possibly even of fraud in the inducement."

"He hasn't pleaded fraud," I said. "Besides, how could he have relied on a number that was too smudged to read?"

"She's admitting the interest rate is indeterminate."

"The interest rate is spelled out in words plain as day," I said.

"It raises a fact question for the jury."

"A jury trial for a suit on a note?" I said. "Your Honor, that would be a complete waste of the court's resources."

The judge said, "I'm inclined to agree with you, Counselor." But he was looking, not at me, but at my opponent over the rims of his glasses.

It was almost more than I could take. "Your

Honor, let's say for the moment that the interest rate could be taken as six and three-eighths. Let's call it that. Resolve the question in the light most favorable to the defendant. The plaintiff is still entitled to judgment for the principal plus six-and-three-eighths."

The judge smiled at me as if I were a precocious child who had misrecited a lesson. "Young lady, if there's a question of fact, there's a question of fact. I can't just pick one set of facts and grant a motion for summary judgment on that basis."

"That's correct, Your Honor," my opponent chimed in.

"That is not correct," I said. "If there is a genuine question of fact, then the jury will either issue a judgment for six-and-three-eighths or six-and-five-eighths. It's not possible that the defendant is going to be any better off than six-and-three-eighths."

"He's entitled to his day in court," my opponent insisted.

"I think that's right." The judge slapped at the bench with his gavel.

"But," I said.

The judge raised his eyebrows. "Young lady, I've already ruled," he said.

I rode down in the elevator with my opponent. He gave me a smile. "You got screwed," he said by way of commiseration.

"You played your part."

"Just doing what I could for a client. He isn't able to pay anything on the note right now, so I had to delay things if I could." He shook his head. "I had no idea it would work."

He obviously hadn't appeared before this judge before. "Probably arguments of counsel sound more persuasive than a young lady's," I said. "That's what gets me. Why are you 'counselor,' and I'm just 'young lady'?"

He made a face and shrugged his shoulders, as if there were no answer to that one.

"I'll add it to my list of things to ask about when we all get to heaven," I said.

"We're not all going."

I looked at him sharply, but he only smiled benignly.

"You're going, I take it," I said as the elevator opened on the ground floor.

"I hope so. 'For the gate is narrow and the way is hard that leads to life, and those who find it are few.'"

"That must be such a comfort to you."

He shrugged, stopping to let me go first through the revolving door. I pushed through and blinked in the strong sunlight.

"You're obviously fit physically and well-trained mentally," he said as he came out behind me.

I decided I didn't like him. "Yeah. So?" I said.

"So what are you doing to train your soul to live in heaven?"

"I haven't thought about it."

His mouth twisted, his eyebrows rose, and he raised a hand with the palm turned up as if in invitation.

"See you," I said. I turned and stalked toward my car, seething with resentment at the turn my life had taken in the last twenty-four hours. My boyfriend had cheated on me, my college teammate was dead, a judge had just made one of the stupidest rulings I could remember, and now I was being presented with the specter of invalidism in the afterlife.

Chapter 11

I didn't even try to get any more work done that day. I went to the police station to be fingerprinted, though I wondered about the wisdom of being so cooperative. The thing that decided me was the thought of Pete Larsen's reaction if the police showed up at the firm to fingerprint one of his lawyers.

Jordan wasn't at the station, but it didn't seem to matter. A fat man with breath that smelled of peppermint rolled my inky fingers on a white card and gave me some goo to clean them with. By five o'clock, about an hour earlier than usual, I had joined the crawl of cars westbound on I-64.

When I got to my neighborhood, I drove along Darby Drive until I spotted the house where I'd head-butted the homeowner before jumping off his tool shed into a trash bin. It was a modest ranch with a brick front. I should probably bake the homeowner some cookies as a token of remorse, I thought.

"Robin, Robin," I said to myself, because I knew I wouldn't do it. I just wasn't the cookie type.

I drove by my own house, reconnoitering before committing myself. There was an old Chevrolet

Caprice I didn't recognize parked on the street about half-a-block away, but no one was in it. I drove around to the alley and pulled into my driveway, triggering my garage door. I pulled in, then got the shivers as the door rumbled down behind my VW Beetle, closing me in.

This sucks, I thought. I got out of the car and swung the car door closed. *Schwoomp*. My pumps made a gritty sound on the garage's cement floor. My hand on the doorknob, I took a breath and opened the door.

It's not often that heart-thumping anticipation precedes anything really bad. The really bad stuff just comes out of nowhere, like my encounter with Misters Mean and Nasty the night before. This time I let myself get worked up, and there was nothing to get worked up about. My house was free of intruders. As nearly as I could tell, it was exactly as I had left it the night before.

I couldn't bring myself to leave the safety of the house to go jogging, though. I tried. I got dressed for it, started out the door, saw that old Caprice still parked against the curb half-a-block away, and stopped. It now looked as if someone was sitting in the car, though from my sidewalk I couldn't have even said male or female. I went back inside.

I did my workout to a DVD, using a stepper I'd gotten at Wal-Mart a year or two before. I kept the volume on the TV low so that if anyone tried to break in, I would hear it. Afterwards, I showered, but briefly, not wanting to become involved in any real-life reenactment of the famous scene from *Psycho*. Instead of my customary T-shirt and panties, I put on a pair of shorts and a running bra I thought might be comfortable enough to sleep in. Just as I finished dressing, the phone rang.

I picked it up. "Hello?"

There was no one there.

"Hello?" I said again.

Breathing. Not heavy breathing, but breathing nonetheless. I listened to it, not saying anything else, and after about half-a-minute the connection ended.

Frowning, I put the receiver back in its cradle, then picked it up again and dialed star-69 to call back my unknown caller.

A man answered. "Hello?" he said uncertainly.

I didn't say anything.

"Hello?" He sounded scared, so to press my advantage I let him hear me breathing. He took it for about ten seconds, then hung up.

Serves him right, I thought, turning away from the phone, but it rang before I'd gone more than a couple of steps. I stopped and stood looking at it. After the fourth ring, my machine picked up, and my recorded message played. "Hi, this is Robin. Leave your name and number, and I'll call you back."

I winced when I heard my name. I was going to have to change the outgoing message.

My caller's breathing came over the speaker. He left me about a minute's worth of it, then hung up. Son of a gun.

I strode to the kitchen, where my phone had Caller ID. I expected the number to be blocked, but it wasn't. The breather's name was Eddie Unger, who was no one I knew. His phone number had the same first three digits as the cell phone I carried in my purse, though, which meant he was calling on a cell phone himself. On a cell phone he could be calling from anywhere. He could be right outside my house.

I turned out the lights and went to the window, but it was dark outside and the shrubbery limited my field of vision. Flipping a light back on, I got out my phone book. Eddie wasn't in it.

"I don't like this," I said aloud.

I put the phone book back in the drawer, then, turning out lights as I went, I walked around the perimeter of the house, looking out the windows, checking the locks, making sure the deadbolts on the doors were engaged. As a substitute for the alarm system I didn't have, I stacked a couple of saucepans by the front and back doors.

A thought occurred to me. I went to the bedroom that served as my office and turned on the computer. After it booted, I went to the web site of the central appraisal district and did a search for E Unger.

There it was. Eddie Unger owned a house on Darby Street, not far from my own house. The picture showed a small ranch house with a brick front.

"Holy cow," I breathed. Eddie Unger was the guy I'd head-butted when he grabbed me from behind.

A smile twisted my face. So Eddie Unger had looked me up and was exacting his revenge. It was a small, warped sort of revenge—most people would have just hired a lawyer—but it was something I thought I understood.

Some fifteen minutes later, I was walking through the dark house one last time in preparation for bed when the phone rang again. For a moment I froze, then I ran back to the kitchen and flipped on a light so I could see the number of the incoming call. It was

Eddie.

I let it ring again, then lifted the receiver to my ear. I didn't say anything.

Neither did my caller.

"You need to stop this, Eddie," I said.

He hung up.

I found myself grinning. Now I could go to bed with some hope of sleeping.

And that's what I did, my cross-trainers by my bed, my keys on the floor beside them.

Chapter 12

A voice by my bed sent me lurching awake, but it was just my clock radio going off as it did every morning at six o'clock. Today, Lady Gaga was singing about the girl she'd met in East L.A. I lay and listened, and gradually my heartbeat returned to normal.

I got to work by seven-thirty and found myself doing catch-up. It was about ten-thirty before I had the chance to place another call to McCormack Labs. This time I used my cell phone.

"Yes, this is Robin Starling with the law firm of Northcutt Hambrick. I'm supposed to meet someone in accounting, but I can't find the right building. Could you…"

"It's the second one on the right as you come in the main entrance."

"And I'm in the right place? Just off West Broad Street out near Goochland?"

"That's right. If you're coming from town, turn right onto McCormack Drive."

"Thank you," I said and hung up.

John Parker was standing in the doorway, his jacket off and the cuffs of his sleeves turned back a couple of times. He was holding a file folder.

"What was that about?" he asked.

"I'm going out to McCormack Labs on my lunch hour."

He came in and sat in one of my client chairs. "I know you don't get the paper," he began, and stopped.

"Wendy Walters is dead," I said.

His eyebrows went up.

"I found the body."

He took a moment to digest that bit of information. "The article in the *Times-Dispatch* didn't mention you," he said finally.

"That's something anyway," I said.

He nodded. "I've got a question for you."

"Okay."

"Where were you the other night, when you saw Wendy at my place? We didn't see you."

"I wasn't waving a flag." I didn't elaborate.

He sighed. "I was just curious. I'm sorry as hell, you know."

"Yes, you are," I conceded.

"Though we didn't actually, uh, complete the transaction. After Wendy went out on the balcony, it was all over."

"Unh huh."

"You don't believe me."

"I don't care."

His head went back. "Oh, wow."

"My sentiments exactly."

He took a deep breath and started to get up, then dropped back into the chair again. "You don't think her murder and the attack on you were related, do you?" he asked.

"Why do you say that?"

"I don't know. There's a lot happening suddenly."

I shrugged. I couldn't disagree with him there.

"Well," he said, levering himself out of the chair again. He went to the door.

"Where did you leave her?" I asked him, my eyes on my pencil holder. "Did you walk her up, or leave her on the sidewalk, or what?" I raised my gaze to his.

"I thought you didn't care."

"John, I found her on the couch with a bloated face and a clothesline around her neck. I'd like to know how such a thing came about."

He was silent.

"Okay, don't tell me," I said. "The police fingerprinted the whole apartment, though. If you were in there, it might be prudent to say so—at least if you're asked officially."

"I walked her up."

I nodded. "She was in her underwear when I found her."

"She had more than that on when I left her."

"Unh huh."

He came back into the office a step. "What did you tell them about me?" he asked.

"Tell whom?"

"The police."

"I didn't tell them anything about you."

"Why not?"

"Why should I? What do they care about you cheating on your girlfriend?"

He was silent for maybe ten seconds. "Thanks."

"If they knew about you," I said, "you'd be the major focus of their investigation, and they need to be focusing on McCormack Labs."

"Wendy's employer?"

"Yesterday, she told me they'd been doing some funny bookkeeping—earnings management or maybe outright fraud."

"And so you like them for murder?"

"It's what I've got. She talks with me about funny business at McCormack Labs. That night I'm assaulted and she's murdered. That seems like quite a coincidence if there's no connection."

He nodded.

"And if you killed her, what was your motive?" I went on. "At worst, you were upset because you didn't get a piece. I don't see that turning into a murderous rage. You never attacked me when I turned you down."

"Did you ever turn me down?"

I made a face at him. The truth was I couldn't remember whether I ever had or not. "Work with me here," I said. "I'm trying to do you a favor."

Chapter 13

Having places to go and people to see, I left early for lunch. I took the Downtown Expressway to I-64 and exited I-64 onto West Broad. Three point two miles later, I turned right onto McCormack, where a wrought-iron fence marked the perimeter of the McCormack Labs complex. A guardhouse sat just inside the open gate. I slowed as a man in a security uniform came out, but he only stretched his back and swung his arms and watched me as I rolled past.

I was in, and the most disturbing thing so far was that the song "Secret Agent Man" kept playing in my head. This just wasn't the kind of thing lawyers did, not any of the ones I knew. For one thing, it was hard to see how I was going to bill anybody three hundred dollars an hour for it.

At 11:45 I pulled into a parking space facing the second building on the right, which, according to my source, housed accounting. It was a flat-roofed, two-story affair. About ten minutes later, people began to exit the building in ones and twos—a tall, thin man with a full head of silver hair, a couple of young men wearing shirts with open collars, a heavy-set black woman. Any or all of them might have worked with Wendy, but I didn't feel like any was a good prospect for developing a quick rapport.

I waited until a woman about my age came out and chirped open a Honda CR-V three cars down from me. She was dressed in what I think of as a little-man suit, a skirt and matching jacket over a cotton shirt that was buttoned to the throat. She was evidently some kind of professional, so, when she pulled out of her parking space, I started my own car and followed her.

She got onto the interstate and off again, then pulled into the parking lot of Regency Square Mall. I parked three rows away from her and hurried after her toward the Dillard's entrance, her thick red hair like a flag bobbing ahead of me. She went to kids' clothing, and I loitered near her, poking through a rack of tops for prepubescent girls while she picked out a natty little outfit for what I figured would be about a four-year-old boy. She paid for it and went out into the mall.

In the food court, she bought a deli sandwich, a bag of chips, and a drink, and she sat down with her tray at a table by herself. The food court was crowded, but I picked a vendor with no line and ended up with a plate of shrimp lo mein and an iced tea. There were a few empty tables, but none right around my target, which was good. I approached her with my tray, and she looked up. She was one of those redheads with a peaches-and-cream complexion and no trace of freckles.

"Hi," I said. "Kind of crowded, isn't it? Do you mind if I sit with you?"

She shrugged her shoulders. "Sure." Her smile was perfunctory.

I pulled out a chair and sat down. "Robin Starling," I said.

It took her several seconds to decide whether she was going to talk to me. "Brooke Marshall," she said finally.

"Work near here?" I took an energetic sip of my tea.

She nodded. "You?"

"No, I'm downtown. Northcutt, Hambrick and Larsen."

"Is that...a law firm, or a group of CPAs, or what?"

"Law firm. We do mostly commercial litigation, but a bit of this and that."

"And you're a lawyer," she said carefully, as if the label might insult me if she got it wrong.

"That's right." I forked shrimp lo mein into my mouth and chewed vigorously. "You?" I had her now, I thought. Once she began asking questions, she could hardly refuse to answer a few of mine.

"I'm a network administrator."

"Computers?"

She nodded. "McCormack Labs. I'm here on my lunch hour buying a present for a little cousin."

I had her volunteering information. "McCormack's the pharmaceutical outfit, isn't it?" I said. "I have a friend who works there. Wendy Walters. I think she's in accounting."

Her face had gone still.

"You know her?" I asked.

She nodded soberly. "I'm in accounting, too."

"She and I went to college together. We played basketball."

She seemed stricken.

"Is something wrong?"

"You haven't seen the paper," she said.

"The newspaper?"

"Wendy Walters is dead." Her voice was soft.

"Dead!" I exclaimed.

"Strangled in her apartment. They found her yesterday."

I stared at her.

"She didn't come in yesterday," Brooke said. "Then today everyone was talking about it."

"But I just tried to call her. I was going to be out this way, and I called to see if she'd meet me for lunch."

Brooke shook her head. For a while we sat in silence, our food forgotten. Then Brooke took a sip of her drink and cleared her throat. "I'm sorry, Robin."

"I just can't believe it."

"For what it's worth, I can't either."

"Did you know her?" I asked.

"Well enough. We've been to lunch."

"I saw her two days ago," I said. "She dropped by my office, and we had smoothies."

Brooke didn't say anything to that.

"She was upset," I said. "I guess maybe she had reason to be."

"She was upset?"

"She seemed to think she'd uncovered some kind of accounting problems there at McCormack, and no one would listen."

"Who wouldn't listen?"

"I don't know. Who would she tell? You?"

"Not me. She might tell Marty Nolen. He's the controller."

"Is he a good guy?"

"I understand he's a good accountant."

"That's a careful response."

She laughed, but the pitch seemed off to me. "Marty's all right," she said. "He's kind of intense sometimes."

"So if there were accounting problems, he'd be all over them."

No response.

"She was nervous as a cat when I saw her," I said. "It was as if she thought someone might be watching her. Has she been like that at work?"

Still nothing, but her own eyes had shifted on me. Her head didn't move, but she seemed to be scanning the people behind me and on both sides of us.

I leaned forward. "She said," I said in a low voice. "She said she had uncovered a second set of books."

Brooke's face jumped as if I'd touched an electrode to her.

"What did she say specifically?" she asked.

"That's just it. She didn't say anything specific."

"Did she give you any details at all?"

I shook my head. "Would it matter? Would details mean anything to you?"

"They might."

"You're an accountant?"

"I was a double major in college, accounting and information systems. I haven't done much with the accounting, except…"

"Except network administration for the accounting department of a Fortune 500 company," I finished for her.

She flushed slightly. "Except that."

"How many of you are there? Network administrators."

"In accounting? I have an assistant, a new hire that started in June."

"And you yourself don't know anything about accounting irregularities or a second set of books?" I said.

Her eyes narrowed.

"Sorry," I said. "All of my conversations tend to devolve into cross-examinations. It's an occupational hazard."

She studied me. "Your running into me here wasn't by chance, was it?" she said.

"I don't think anything happens by chance, really. Do you?"

"No," she said. "I don't." She stood up and walked away, leaving her tray on the table, her food unfinished.

I watched her go, realizing I had blown it. For a few minutes, I'd had the perfect contact inside the accounting department at McCormack, and I had blown it.

"Crap," I said.

Chapter 14

I got some work done that afternoon and didn't knock off until seven. When I did, I went by the Y and joined a pickup game of basketball with a couple of guys I'd played with before and one I hadn't. They were all taller and heavier than I was, and they tended to move me around under the basket, but I did all right for myself. Teamed with the new guy, I scored six of our eight baskets before the other team got its tenth and the game was over.

When men play basketball, I've noticed, they produce sweat like fire hydrants produce water, and I was no summer daisy myself. We split up, going to our respective locker rooms. I think there was a Yoga class going on that night. Women all around me were putting on Spandex as I changed out of my gym shorts and my sleeveless T.

The old Chevy Caprice was parked across the street from my house again, and there was someone behind the wheel. I pulled up beside it and triggered the window on the passenger side of my Beetle. The man in the Caprice glanced at me and then looked away, shielding his face with his left hand. I waited.

Finally, he lowered his hand, and his window went down. He had a round face and limp black hair. His nose was black and purple from where I'd hit him, but I thought he might be twenty-five.

"Are you Eddie Unger?" I asked.

He shook his head almost violently, but what he said was, "How did you know?"

"A hunch. I'm sorry about knocking you down at your house the other night."

He nodded jerkily. "I know you are. It's all right."

"Then what are you doing here?"

"I thought…" He broke off.

"Yes?"

"I thought you might want to go out with me some time."

I tried to take it in stride. "You need to work on your approach," I said.

"I mean, it's like we know each other. You know?"

I supposed he meant that I'd been to his house, and he'd had his arms around me.

"It's more like we're complete strangers," I said.

His mouth twisted, and I was afraid for a moment he was going to cry.

"I'll tell you what," I said. "I'm in the middle of a crisis right now at work, but when things settle down, I'll bake you some cookies." Somehow.

He sat up straighter. "Really?"

"Yes. But for right now you've got to stop stalking me, okay?"

He nodded.

"We have a deal?"

"Sure."

"Great." I put my window back up, gave him what I meant to be a friendly wave, then drove around to my garage. When I went out the front door to get my mail, his car was gone. I checked my watch and gave a nod of satisfaction.

Before I went to bed, I did another perimeter-check. This time, already more comfortable in my own home, I didn't bother with the gym clothes and the shoes by the bed. I changed into my usual T-shirt and panties, got a bottle of water from the fridge, and set it on the nightstand, something I'd neglected to do the day before.

I drink my first water of the day before getting up in the morning. No doubt it's one of those weird rituals that single women develop, but six half-liter bottles a day keep me feeling lubricated, and, if I don't start off with one, it's hard to get them in.

I threw back the covers and got in bed, pulling up just the sheet for covers. In the summer, as a good citizen of Planet Earth and a miserly young woman besides, I keep the house at a warm 76 degrees. Just before I dropped off, I glanced over at the clock. It was 10:35.

Chapter 15

2:41. I lay still, my heart pounding, my eyes moving over the shadows, picking out the dark dresser, the straight-backed chair, the low shelf of books that looked black against the cream-colored walls. Everything looked as it should, yet my ears strained in the silence for some repetition of the sound that had brought me out of sleep.

Nothing came. It occurred to me that the sound might have been part of the dream that I couldn't quite remember. The thin layer of perspiration that made my skin feel tacky suggested the dream had not been a peaceful one.

Just as I was selling myself on the only-a-dream theory, there was a creak from somewhere in the house, a soft groan of wood. I swung my legs out of bed. It's the house settling, said the practical, sensible voice inside me, but my heart was racing, and I knew I was never going to get back to sleep until I checked it out.

Without turning on any lights, I padded out of the master bedroom into the hall. I looked into bedroom number two, then into the bathroom on the right and into the living room through the archway on the left. Bedroom number three, which I used as my study, was at the end of the hall. A little light filtered in through the front window, showing everything in its proper place.

My heartbeat was returning to normal as I went out into the rest of the house. All was as it should be in the living room. The front door was closed and locked. Nothing looked out of place in the kitchen. The back door was secure.

Just an excitable girl, I murmured as I headed back to the bedroom, but I wasn't too hard on myself. With all that had happened, I thought I was entitled to be a little jumpy. I was reaching for my bed, already feeling the soft mattress in my imagination and the luxury of my spine relaxing a vertebra at a time, when something hard and thin closed around my throat and jerked me backward, almost off my feet. There was a shape behind me. I thrashed desperately in an effort to dislodge it, and together we staggered about the dark bedroom, taking out a floor lamp and knocking over the bookcase, crashing into the dresser, into the doorway, into the wall. I couldn't get at my attacker, and, despite my struggles, the cord remained around my throat, just under my chin, completely closing off the flow of air.

The darkness of the room began to take on a grayish quality, and a high-pitched whistle sounded from somewhere. I curled my legs off the ground, inspired by some crazy notion of getting to my attacker's head with my feet. There was no chance of that—for one thing, my own head was mostly in the way—but it turned out to be the best thing I could have done, maybe the only thing. My attacker wasn't prepared to take my weight, and he staggered forward, unable to support it. He went to his knees, dropping me down onto the base of my spine, but the pressure on my neck disappeared as he lurched over me, his hips above my face and his head above my thighs. I reached up with my knees and clamped them against his head, locking my bare feet together as the air flowed sweet and clean into my lungs. I gagged and turned my head to the side just as the man surged upward, but I managed to keep my grip on his head, my knees pressing into his neck just below his jaw. When he fell back, his crotch mashed painfully into my face, and he tried again, dragging my legs and lower body with him as he rose. Desperately, I clung to his head with my knees, arching my body in an effort to drive him back down, and this time his head thudded solidly into the hardwood flooring. We thrashed on the floor like a pair of rough lovers, the rough fabric of his pants grinding against my face as he tried to break free, me holding onto his head with my knees even as I pushed at his hips with hands and forearms in a desperate effort to keep him off my face enough so I could breathe.

It wasn't working. I couldn't get enough air. In desperation, I stopped pushing at him. I grabbed him about the hips with both arms, pushed my face into his crotch, and bit down.

He jerked violently, but I held on as he thrashed and screamed frantic, breathless screams that sounded horrifyingly inhuman. He twisted and jerked and rolled, and I held on with arms and legs and teeth. There was blood in my mouth—I knew with horror that it was his—and I still couldn't breathe. I opened my mouth, releasing his inseam, pushing at his hips, twisting and rolling in a blind effort to get out from under him, but as his body twisted away from me, I felt a muffled crack between my knees, felt it or heard it as his body rolled over one leg and he fell mostly on his back. Panicked, I opened my knees, letting go of his head, and finally was able to scramble out from under him.

I scooted backwards on hands and feet, gasping, until I came up against the bed and stopped. I could see the body only in shadow, but the head was canted sideways at an impossible angle and nothing was moving. I scrambled onto my bed, my eyes fixed on the corpse on my bedroom floor. The clock on my nightstand read 2:49, which added to my sense of unreality, of having come unmoored in time and space. Unless my clock had stopped, it had been only eight minutes since I'd gone in search of the noise that had awakened me. I reached for the phone, keeping a careful watch on the body of the man who had attacked me.

The body moved.

With a yelp I leaped off my bed, skipping past him, and running full tilt into the doorjamb. I bounced and kept going. Somehow I got out of the room and into the hall and then into the living room. My impressions were disjointed, as if I were teleporting from place to place rather than moving through the intervening space. Finding myself in the kitchen, I snatched up the cordless phone from its cradle and, dropping down behind the counter, punched the talk button, then 9-1-1. I put the phone to my ear.

Nothing. I thought for one panicky instant that I was doing something wrong, that under the stress of the moment I had forgotten how to use my own telephone. I pushed END, then TALK again, and put the phone to my ear to hear the dial tone, but there was none. I straightened, looking in the direction of my bedroom, where I'd left my cell. There was a man on the far side of my living room, visible only in silhouette. He just stood there, unmoving, his head cocked to one side as if he were listening. I could hear myself breath.

He moved, and I threw the phone at him. It was a good, straight throw, but it missed him by about three feet and thudded into the wall.

"Crap," I said.

He was coming. I yanked out a drawer, and it fell to the floor amid a clatter of tableware and utensils. I yanked at another one and overdid it on that one, too. Tossing the drawer aside, I scanned the dark floor with eyes and fingers for something I could use as a weapon—an ice pick, a knife of some kind.

I'd pulled out the wrong drawers. All I saw among the ladles and spatulas and whatnots was a corkscrew, just a wooden handle and a short spiral of steel. It would have to do. I snatched it up and scooted around the counter, bending double to avoid being seen. Standing, I pressed myself against the wall next to the doorway, the corkscrew tight in my hand, the steel twisting out between my fingers.

A lamp crashed to the floor in the living room. Silence. I waited, ears straining, every muscle in my body tensed and ready.

When he came through the doorway, he was like a man in a trance, moving unsteadily, his head lolling on his right shoulder. I stepped into him, sliding one arm about his waist and driving for his kidney with the corkscrew protruding from my fist.

It went in surprisingly easily, as if I were punching into a balloon filled with Jell-O. His body stiffened briefly, and he collapsed.

I backed out of the kitchen into the living room, my eyes on the man's body. I could hear him breathing. It was a horrible gasping sound, but I didn't trust him to stay down. When I lost sight of him, I turned and ran for the front door, my fingers scrabbling for the thumb latch, for the chain, for the doorknob.

The hot, humid air of an August night in Virginia felt to me like airy freedom. I ran down the sidewalk to the street and crossed it, hobbling slightly on my bare feet.

Chapter 16

There was no question, really, of where to go. I crossed the street and rang the bell of a retired physician who lived by himself. In the evenings he was often outside tending his yard or sitting on his front steps. Once after my evening jog I'd been sitting on his steps chatting with him while he weeded his rosebushes, when a woman stopped her Lincoln Continental in the middle of Beechnut Street, got out, and strode over to us, her heels tapping on the sidewalk.

"You do nice work," she said to Dr. McDermott.

He squinted up at her and told her thank you. It was a crisp, spring evening, and he was wearing a stained, white flannel shirt under bib-overalls.

"How much do you charge?"

"Pardon?"

"For yard work. Do you charge by the hour or by the job or what?" There wasn't a strand of gray in her blonde hair, though her time-weathered face said she was sixty and her elegant coiffure made me think of old issues of *Life* magazine.

Dr. McDermott sat on his heels blinking up at her, looking bemused.

"Well?" she asked him.

"He does my yard in exchange for sexual favors," I said. "It's a very satisfactory arrangement for both of us."

The woman's head jerked toward me, her cheeks sucking in and her mouth puckering in a way that was distinctly fishlike. I smiled brightly, and her eyes went back to Dr. McDermott, who shrugged and lifted his eyebrows.

Her mouth closed in a firm line, and she spun on her two-and-a-half-inch heel and tapped back down the sidewalk. Her car door slammed, her engine roared, and she was gone.

Embarrassed now that the two of us were by ourselves, I gave Dr. McDermott an apologetic smile. "Sorry, I shouldn't have butted in," I said. "It just sort of came out."

"You do have a free way of talking," he said.

"I hope I didn't embarrass you."

He shook his head. "It takes more than a free way of talking to embarrass me."

"And she had it coming," I said.

It probably took Dr. McDermott less than two minutes to get to the door, but it felt like too long. I stood watching my house. No sign of anything going on there, but as the adrenalin seeped from my system I started to shake. I needed to sit down soon, or Dr. McDermott would be picking me out of his rosebushes.

The porch light flashed on and the door whooshed open behind me, causing me to spin around so fast I nearly turned myself inside out.

"Robin Starling?" Dr. McDermott said.

I stretched my mouth at him, trying to smile. "There's a man inside my house." I stopped, shocked at the hoarse quality of my voice, then said, "I was hoping I could use your phone."

He looked toward my house, which still showed no sign of activity or of anything amiss. His eyes came back to me, a thirty-year-old woman in a T-shirt and panties standing on his doorstep in the middle of the night. My eyes had sprung a leak, and, noticing it, he stepped back, reaching out a hand to draw me inside.

"What man is in your house?" he asked, closing the door and bolting it behind me.

"He tried to...to kill me." It sounded melodramatic, especially in my newly acquired smoker's voice, but I couldn't help it, and my tears began in earnest. Dr. McDermott put his arms around me, and it wasn't long before my chest was hitching and my tears were steaming in an all-out cry. I found that I derived an irrational amount of comfort from his patting my back and telling me that everything was going to be all right.

When the worst of the storm had passed, he put me in a chair in the kitchen and picked up the wall phone to dial 9-1-1.

"Yes," he said. "This is Donald McDermott. I live at...Yes, that's right. A young lady who lives across the street tells me there is an intruder in her home...No, she's here. She seems to be all right." He raised his eyebrows at me, and I nodded. He had a tuft of hair standing straight up on the top of his balding head, drawing a watery smile from me through what remained of my tears.

"Her house number is ten-seventeen. Yes, thank you." He looked at me when he had hung up. "They have a patrol car in the area," he said.

I nodded.

He poured me a glass of water from a plastic jug in the refrigerator and set it in front of me. "Drink that. I'd make you some tea or something, but it sounds like they're right around the corner. Will you be all right?"

"I think so." I tried to take a sip of the water, but it hurt to swallow. My hand went to my bruised throat.

Dr. McDermott said, "Let me see if I can find you something to wear before the police get here. Your nightshirt just barely covers your..." He made a flapping gesture with his hand. "I'll be right back."

I looked down. *Just barely* was politeness on his part; even seated, half my underwear was showing. My face got hot, and, when Dr. McDermott came back with a white, terry cloth bathrobe, I shrugged into it gratefully.

"There," he said. "All better."

We heard the sound of a car engine out front, followed by the slamming of doors. Dr. McDermott peered out through his blinds. "They're here," he said.

There were two of them, one about fifty and one much younger. We came out onto the front porch as they approached, and they stopped at the edge of it. "You the ones called about an intruder?" the older cop asked.

Dr. McDermott nodded. He opened his mouth to elaborate, but I beat him to it.

"My name is Robin Starling," I croaked. "I live

right over there. I woke to a noise about…a half-hour ago. There was a man in the house. He tried to strangle me with some kind of cord."

"Is he still there?"

"I think so." I swallowed. "He's probably pretty badly injured, and he may be…" I swallowed again.

"Yes?"

"Dead," I said, and cleared my throat.

The older cop quirked his mouth at me. "How did that happen?" he asked.

"I think I broke his neck."

"How…"

"And then I stabbed him in the kidney with a corkscrew."

Their eyes shifted to Dr. McDermott, then came back to me.

"Do you have your keys, ma'am?"

"I ran out without them. It shouldn't be locked."

"You wait here. We'll go have a look."

Dr. McDermott and I sat down on his front porch steps as we watched them cross the street. I was hugging the bathrobe around me, chilled, though the outside temperature was probably somewhere in the eighties.

"You've had a rough night," Dr. McDermott said.

I nodded, dumbly. I doubted I could live through a worse one.

Chapter 17

In about fifteen minutes the cops were back. According to their nametags, the older one was named Aston; the younger one, Phillips.

"You want to come with us?" Aston said.

Dr. McDermott stood with me. "What is it?" he asked.

"We'd like to walk through the house with Ms. Sterling."

"Starling," I said.

"Is he dead, then?" Dr. McDermott asked.

"If you don't mind, we'd like to address that question when we get back inside the house."

"Don't you think that's going to be unnecessarily traumatic for...?" He jerked his head in my direction.

"Ms. Sterling," I said. My stores of fear and shock and horror seemed to be exhausted, and I felt strangely cheerful, as if I had some kind of bipolar disorder and was swinging back toward the manic pole.

"We're afraid it's necessary," Phillips said to Dr. McDermott.

"Perhaps you'd like to come with her," Aston suggested.

"Thank you, I will," he said.

The four of us crossed the street together. The front door was standing open. The cops entered the house ahead of Dr. McDermott and me, turning toward the kitchen, and we followed. I reached out and took hold of one of Dr. McDermott's slightly gnarled hands.

Just inside the kitchen, blood was smeared and puddled on the floor, and a bloody handprint was on the counter. On the jamb of the door leading out to the garage was another smear of blood, and through the open doorway I could see through the garage to the alley.

"There're blood spots all the way down the alley to the street," Phillips said.

"There's a lot of it right here," I said.

"Too much," Dr. McDermott added.

"What do you mean?" asked Phillips.

"I mean he lost a lot of blood to have walked away under his own power."

"You a doctor?" Phillips said.

Dr. McDermott nodded. "I am."

"Let's go in the bedroom," Aston said.

My room was a wreck—a tangle of bedclothes trailing off onto the floor, a smashed lamp, an overturned nightstand with stuff spilling from its drawer…A strong floral scent came from a perfume bottle that had broken when it fell from the dresser. Amid the clutter was a length of what looked like clothesline, about a yard of it.

"He tried to strangle me with that cord there," I said, pointing.

Dr. McDermott looked at my neck. "I have something for that back at the house," he said.

"What happened?" Aston said to me.

"I heard a noise. It woke me up, and..." I had to pause to clear my throat, making a noise like the grinding of gears. "I got up to walk through the house and make sure everything was all right."

"Unh huh," Aston said.

"Everything seemed okay. I came back to the bedroom, and suddenly this man was behind me and a cord was around my neck."

"How did you get away?"

I described it as best I could. When I got to the scissors-lock I got on my attacker's head, everybody's eyes went to my legs, which thanks to the bathrobe were only visible below the knee. I described the muffled snap I'd heard when he twisted and fell and the unnatural angle of his head. "His head was still cocked on one side when he came out of the bedroom. He was just this shadow moving across the living room. With his head tilted that way, he...It was like one of those zombie movies."

I looked from face to face, but got no encouragement.

"The phone was dead," I went on. "I got a corkscrew out of one of the drawers, and, when he came into the kitchen, I stabbed him with it. It was right where we saw all that blood. He fell and was still gasping and choking when I went out the front door and ran across the street to Dr. McDermott's."

"You said he was dead," Phillips said.

"Well, dying. I don't see how he...I don't know."

Nobody said anything, and I wasn't at all sure how to interpret their silence.

"But that cord on the floor looks just like the cord that was found around the neck of Wendy Walters," I said.

The name didn't seem to register.

"The woman who was murdered in Shockoe Bottom," I said.

Three sets of eyebrows climbed three foreheads.

"What about her?" Aston asked.

"I'm the one who found the body." My throat was hurting and my back was beginning to cramp up on me. "Could I get some water?" I said. "I'm not feeling so good."

Dr. McDermott got the water for me, along with four Advil from the cabinet over my sink. It was more than I'd ever taken before, but he was the doctor.

We sat in the living room. Aston asked a few more questions, and Phillips scribbled in his notebook. "I'd feel a lot better about this if you could give us a better description of your attacker," Aston said.

"It was dark. He was behind me. When I finally saw him from the front, he was just a shadow on the other side of the living room."

"A shadow with its head cocked on one side."

"Yes."

"Height?"

I shook my head. "My height, a little taller."

"How tall would that be?"

"Five-eleven."

"So you think he was…"

"Somewhere between five-ten and maybe six-four or so."

Aston rolled his eyes.

After a while, some police technicians came and scraped up the blood, or some of it. There were no usable prints, as it turned out. Even the handprint on the counter had evidently been made by a latex glove.

When everyone had gone, Dr. McDermott said, "Get your keys. Or your purse or whatever. You're spending the rest of the night at my house."

"That's all right. I can go to a hotel."

"Not tonight. You need me to doctor those abrasions around your neck, for one thing, check you out and make sure nothing's damaged."

"Thank you," I said.

"I have a guest room all made up. You'll even have your own bathroom."

Chapter 18

I woke to the smell of bacon. The room was cool, but, though the bedspread was on the floor, and the sheet was in a twist, I was damp with perspiration. I swung my legs out of bed and sat waiting for my breathing to slow, feeling more exhausted than I had when I lay down. I sighed and got up and swung my arms. A few circles with them, forward and backward, took out some of the stiffness, but it was going to be a long day.

It was while I was using the bathroom that my nightmare came back to me, dark shapes with canted heads chasing me down doorless corridors that went on and on forever. A shudder went through me, and I did my best to push the images away and slam the door on them.

After shrugging into Dr. McDermott's terrycloth robe, I padded barefoot down to the kitchen, which was too bright and sharp-edged to seem quite real. There was a Cuisinart coffee maker sputtering the final drops of coffee into the carafe, bacon sizzling on a hot frying pan, and Dr. McDermott standing over the stove in an apron decorated with a grinning pig's head.

He motioned me to the table. "How's the throat?"

"All right." The words came out in an unexpected croak, though, and I touched my neck. It was tender.

"Some coffee will feel good on it. How do you take it?" He put down his spatula and got a couple of mismatched mugs from a cabinet.

"Black," I said.

"Me, too." He poured and brought the mugs. "Let me get the bacon off the fire, and we'll sit a bit," he said.

I took a sip of the coffee. It was flavored with something I couldn't identify, but it was wonderful and it felt good going down.

Dr. McDermott brought a plate of bacon with him to the table. "Did you sleep well?"

I shook my head. "Nightmares."

He nodded as if he had expected it.

"Zombies like the one from last night," I said by way of explanation. .

"Brains," he croaked, and in response to my uncertain expression added, "*Night of the Living Dead.* A movie. You probably wouldn't have seen it."

"What bothers me, it's not the first time the supernatural has broken in on me lately." I told him about finding Wendy's body and the sense I'd had that she was there in the room with me. "I mean her, herself, not just her corpse. Before that, when I was down in the street, there was a moment when I thought I saw the window blinds move as if someone were looking out through them."

"Maybe someone was. Her killer?"

I shook my head decisively. "Couldn't have been.

There was no way for him to have gotten out." Though, now that I thought about it, I wondered. I had spent a lot of time on the balcony, and the door to the apartment was around the corner.

"We are surrounded by the invisible," Dr. McDermott said.

"What?"

"Love, fear, hope. Things with no physical substance that nonetheless are very real."

"Yes, but…This is different. Love and fear and hope don't have personality. They're just feelings."

"You don't believe that. Is friendship just something inside you? Is courage just an emotional state, or is it something real, something important?"

I seemed to remember something about this from my freshman philosophy class, but I hadn't paid much attention.

"People have often attributed personality to love and hate," Dr. McDermott said.

I shook my head.

"God, Cupid. The devil," he said.

I smiled a little. "You remind me of a lawyer I ran into a couple of days ago. Out of nowhere he started talking to me about how prepared was I for the afterlife."

"Sorry."

"No, it's okay. Things just seem to come in waves, that's all."

He stood. "I'll put on the eggs."

It was late morning before Dr. McDermott and I went back to my house. I was freshly showered, and my stomach was still warm from a breakfast of bacon and eggs and Pillsbury biscuits.

"What a mess," Dr. McDermott said. We were in the kitchen. The lab techs had cleaned up the worst of the blood and the worst of their own mess, but ServiceMaster they were not.

"What's that smell?" I asked. "It's not…"

"Don't ask."

As unpleasant as the odor in the kitchen was, the heavy scent of perfume in my bedroom was almost as bad. "I'll wait for you in the living room," Dr. McDermott said. "Then see you off in your car."

"Thank you." Though my nightmare had by that time dissipated like morning fog, I got my clothes on as quickly as possible. I was running late for work, very late.

Despite my best efforts, it was nearly ten when I got to the office, and the red light on my phone was glowing, indicating I had missed some calls. As I took my seat, I hit the message button on my phone and punched in my password.

Five new messages, the first from John Parker at 8:45 that morning: "Robin, where the hell are you? You're not at home, and you're not here. I'll try your cell."

Message number two, also from John Parker: "Why do you even have a cell phone if you're not going to keep it turned on?"

Message number three: "Okay, so you're out somewhere. When you get back…Never mind, I don't think you can call me here."

Message number four: "I'm at the Richmond Police Department. Headquarters. I'm…They're holding me for Wendy Walters's murder. Get down here as soon as you can, will you?"

Message number five was from Pete Larsen, the

law firm's senior partner. He wanted to see me; he didn't say what about.

I punched the speaker button to disconnect. "Oh boy," I said to no one in particular. John didn't need me; he needed a criminal defense lawyer. Tom Mitchell, one of the firm's partners, had begun his legal career as a prosecutor. I thought about taking this to him, but John could have called Mitchell himself if he'd wanted to.

I drummed my fingers on my credenza. It seemed there was nothing for it but to get down to police headquarters. I stood up. The phone began to ring as I left the office, but I let it ring. If it was John, I was on my way. If it was Larsen, he was going to have to wait.

Chapter 19

It didn't take long to get to John Parker. Ten minutes to the station. Less time than that before Ray Hernandez came down to the lobby and took me up. Ray was Jordan's partner. I'd seen him before, at Wendy's apartment, though I hadn't spoken to him.

On the second floor we came to a line of numbered doors. Hernandez rapped on one marked "2," and James Jordan came out wearing a short-sleeve shirt and a tie that was obviously a clip-on.

"It is you," he said.

I couldn't deny it.

"I didn't figure there could be two Robin Starlings practicing law in Richmond. It was just hard to believe it when Parker said he was calling you."

"We're associates in the same firm." My voice sounded almost back to normal, which was a relief.

"It seems like too much of a coincidence, somehow," Jordan said.

"Maybe. Depends on why you've arrested John Parker. You have arrested him, haven't you?"

"Yes."

"Have you charged him?"

"We're still talking to him. We've just had him in custody since seven o'clock this morning. What happened to your neck?"

My hand went halfway to my throat before I stopped it. "Last night someone broke into my house and tried to strangle me with a piece of clothesline."

"What?" He looked incredulous.

"Seems like too much of a coincidence, too, doesn't it?"

"Where do you live?"

"West end. Halfway to Short Pump. There should be a police report."

"They get him?"

"The guy who attacked me? No. He got away."

"It wasn't Parker, I take it."

"No, but I like how your mind works."

"You mean, suspecting Parker?"

"No. In realizing the attack on me has to be connected to Wendy's murder."

"How?"

"How should I know? If I had the resources of the Richmond Police Department, I'm thinking maybe I could find out enough to connect the dots."

"What dots do you think need connecting?"

"Isn't it obvious?"

"Humor me."

"Okay, dot one. Wendy Walters comes to see me and gives me a disc. Dot two: Hours later, two men accost me outside my home, and Wendy's data disc goes missing. Dot three, later that same night Wendy is strangled with a piece of clothesline. Then two nights after that, someone tries to do the same thing to me."

"That would be dot four?"

"Dot four," I said.

Hernandez said, "Are you sure it was clothesline they used on you?"

I nodded. "About a yard of white clothesline."

"With Walters it was telephone wire," he said.

"What?"

"A gray telephone wire."

"I remember white."

"You were pretty upset," Jordan said. His voice was gentle, but I looked back and forth between them, wondering if they were jerking me around. They seemed sincere, but then they were cops in a murder investigation.

"So what have you got on John Parker?" I said.

"Is he going to talk to us?"

The question suggested he hadn't already, which seemed like good news. "I don't know," I said. "What have you got on him?"

"We're supposed to ask the questions."

"I'm supposed to advise my client, and I need some basis for doing it. You didn't just pick him up at random. Come on."

Jordan ran his tongue along the inside of his cheek. "Fingerprints," he said finally. "His inside her apartment and now hers inside his."

"How did you happen to have his prints for comparison?"

"Computer kicked him out. Attorneys are fingerprinted when they're licensed."

I remembered. What I hadn't realized was that the prints became available to law enforcement. "So why did you need me to drive over here to give you my prints?" I asked.

"Convenience. Make sure we had them."

Obviously, he wasn't talking about *my* convenience. "And that's what you've got on John? Fingerprints?"

"And a witness who saw them downtown together the day Walters was killed. She called us after Wendy's picture appeared in the paper."

"She knew John Parker by name," Hernandez interjected. "Works in the same building, says he hit on her once."

That would be John.

"We'll have DNA evidence in forty-eight hours," Jordan said. "Victim had intercourse almost immediately before she died." With that, he opened the door on Interrogation Room 2, where John Parker sat in a wrinkled T-shirt, his folded hands on the table in front of him.

I stepped inside.

"Let us know when you're ready," Jordan said, and he closed the door behind me.

I stood looking down at John, and he looked back at me.

"I could swear you told me you never consummated your relationship with Wendy," I said finally. "'Didn't close the transaction'—weren't those your words?"

He took a breath and let it out again, then shrugged. "It was what you needed to hear—what I needed for you to hear, anyway. I hardly expected forensic science to contradict me."

I sat across from him, thumped my purse down on the table and slapped my legal pad down beside it. I knew it was time to let go of the merely personal, but I was having trouble doing it. "Of course I lied to you, Robin," I said in a deep voice that was meant to mimic his. "How could I know I was going to get caught?"

"Would it help to tell you I was sorry?"

"For what? The lying or the infidelity?"

"You choose."

I shook my head. "A little genuine contrition might help, but I'm afraid the word *sorry* has lost its pizzazz."

He turned his hands palms up. "Maybe this was a mistake," he said.

"If you mean calling me to get you out of jail, of course it's a mistake. Tom Mitchell is the obvious choice."

"I'd rather keep this quiet if I can. This is so obviously some kind of mix-up."

"Does that mean you've been answering questions? To clear up the obvious mix-up?"

"I'm not an idiot."

The point was, perhaps, debatable, but I let it go. "Good," I said. The explanations of the accused were admissible as evidence. Too often, innocent people tried to explain their way out of difficulty, but succeeded only in supplying the police with the one bit of evidence they could have obtained from no other source.

John said, "So what do we do? If I don't say anything, they're going to charge me."

"They might let you go while they wait for the DNA evidence."

He winced.

"It is your DNA, I take it?"

"Yes, it's my DNA. It's my DNA, all right?"

"Was it your telephone wire, too?"

"What?"

"The wire around her neck. Did you strangle her?"

"No, I didn't strangle her. I told you that."

I wasn't sure he had, but I said, "Would that have been part of the same conversation in which you denied having intercourse?"

He didn't say anything.

I raised a hand. "I'll let it go. It's not like I believed you in the first place."

"What do you mean, you didn't believe me?"

"Save the outrage. Liars aren't entitled to it. What I mean is that men are unreliable where their hormones are concerned, so I try not to rely on them."

He took a breath, then shrugged. "So what do we do now?"

"If you strangled her, then you shouldn't say anything," I said. "They'll charge you, or they won't. They'll prove their case against you if they can."

"But if I'm innocent?"

"I don't know. What have they got on you? They've got you downtown with her on the day of her death. They've got her inside your apartment, and they've got you inside hers. And, of course, they've got you having sex with her."

"What else do they need?"

"I'm sure they'd like to have your prints on the murder weapon."

"The telephone wire? They won't have that."

"So what they have is opportunity. What they don't have is motive. Without that, I think they've got to do more than prove you had opportunity. They've got to show you were the only one with opportunity."

"To do that, they'd have to show I was in her apartment when she died. They can't narrow down time of death like that."

"You think?" It was what I thought, too, but I was operating way outside my area of specialization.

"Even if they could," John said, "they'd need a witness who'd clocked my coming and going."

I looked at him, thinking. Finally, I said, "I'm over my head, John. What you need is a criminal defense lawyer with a team of investigators going around talking to the neighbors to see if any of them saw somebody else entering or leaving that apartment. You need your own forensics expert to challenge what the police have on time of death. You need to remain silent until your lawyer knows exactly what their case is—and probably all the way through trial. You need all kinds of things, and I don't even know what all of them are."

"You finished?"

"I'm finished."

"Three things, Robin. Money. Reputation. Time." He raised a finger. "I haven't got the money for the kind of three-ring circus you're talking about." He raised another finger. "If I spend the next several months as a murder suspect, I'll never practice law in this town again. Three, I can't afford the time. If I'm in jail for any time at all, I'm going to be out of a job."

He seemed to have devoted some thought to it.

"So what do you want from me?" I asked.

"You remember when we first came to the firm, how you and I got all the call-in clients?"

"And the walk-ins." My favorite had been a fifty-year-old man who wanted to sue Fruit-of-the-Loom because he thought his jockey shorts had made him impotent.

John said, "One of my call-ins was an employee of one of the firm's corporate clients, a blue collar guy who was calling us because he knew we were the company's lawyers. He'd been arrested for drunk driving, and the police wanted him to take a sobriety test, one of those things where he walks along a straight line and climbs some steps and so on."

"Didn't they have the results of a breathalyzer test?"

John frowned. "I can't remember. Maybe he refused it. That's not the point. The point is, I was a new lawyer, what did I know? I told him if they wanted him to take the test, I guess he had to take it."

"Good grief."

"Then I got on the phone to a criminal defense lawyer on the firm's referral list. I was feeling terrible at that point—I'd just given legal advice over the phone, and I didn't know what I was talking about. The criminal defense lawyer…"

"Who was it?"

"I can't remember. Anyway, he told me that if the client didn't feel drunk, it was probably okay for him to take the test."

It suddenly seemed like I'd heard the story before. "I thought he said that ordinarily he advised clients not to take any tests," I said.

"Well, he did say that. But when I told him what I'd done, he said it was probably all right. That when people don't feel drunk, they can usually touch their noses and climb stairs and all that without too much of a problem."

"And this guy did."

"That's right. He passed the test, and the D.A. ultimately abandoned the case."

I could see why. If the police had wanted him to take the test, they must have thought the test was valid: *If he had failed the test, officer, wouldn't that suggest that his blood alcohol was high? So, since he passed the test, doesn't that suggest that his blood alcohol was not high? Has the test been validated, or hasn't it, officer? Is the Richmond Police Department in the habit of giving drunk-tests that don't mean anything?* It would have been a tough case to prosecute.

"So what's the point?" I said. "They're not asking you to take a drunk-test."

"The point is, I'm innocent, so ultimately the facts will bear me out. I don't have the time or the money to develop the facts. The police department does."

"That would be nice if the police department had your interests at heart. But once you're a suspect, what the police are going to be looking for are incriminating facts, not exculpatory facts."

"Facts are facts."

"So you want to talk to the police?"

"I think I have to. I know about what time I left her apartment, and that might help them narrow down the time of death. She talked to you about accounting scandals, but I was the one who saw her looking out windows and jumping at noises. Between the two of us, we can show that she was scared to death and we can show why. We might get the police looking in a more useful direction."

"It sounds like you've made your decision."

"I think I have."

"Then what am I here for? You want me to tell you you're doing the right thing?"

"I want your help. This is going to be the cross-examination of my life, and I'm on the wrong side of it."

I studied him.

"Okay," I said.

"Okay?"

"Okay." I didn't know if talking to the police was a good idea or not, but John was the client and it was his decision. I got up and banged on the door.

Chapter 20

I sat next to John on the side of the table farthest from the door. Jordan and Hernandez sat across from us. Jordan and I both had legal pads. Hernandez put a small tape recorder in the middle of the table and turned it on.

"Okay, shoot," Jordan said to John Parker.

I said, "I'd think we'd rather proceed by question and answer."

"Did you kill Wendy Walters?" Hernandez asked John.

"No."

"I'm sure that's a load off your mind," I said.

"What do you mean by that crack?" Jordan asked me.

"I was thinking you'd be more interested in specifics."

"Okay." He said to John, "When did you first meet Wendy Walters?"

"Monday morning. I saw her in Robin's office."

"That would be Robin Starling, your attorney?"

"That's right." In response to further questions, John told him about Wendy calling him to go home with her to check out her apartment, then driving him out to his.

Hernandez said, "She suggest going to your place?"

"Yes. We were at her apartment, but she decided she didn't want to go up."

"She wanted to go to your place."

"That's what I said. She was scared."

"That's why she wanted you to go home with her in the first place. She was scared," Hernandez said.

"Yes. Evidently, she thought someone might be there. She wanted me, or someone, with her while she checked it out."

"But she didn't check it out."

"No, when it came to it, she was too scared to go in at all."

"She told you she was scared, or she seemed scared?"

"She wanted someone to go with her into her own apartment. Obviously, she was scared about something."

"But she didn't tell you what," Hernandez said. I didn't like the way this was going. Hernandez was making statements and inviting John to contradict him. It gave him too much power to direct John's statement.

"No," John said in answer to the nonquestion. "I understand she told Robin what she was scared of earlier in the day. And that she tried to get hold of Robin before she called me."

I felt Jordan's eyes on me, but I didn't look at him.

John said, "So we got to my place, and things... progressed. We were getting along pretty well. Then a dog started barking in the next building, and she just came completely unwound."

"What do you mean by that?"

John gave him specifics, Wendy insisting he go to the balcony to take a look, then going out onto the balcony herself, then going to the peephole in the front door to check that out, and so on. She never settled down again. Eventually, she wanted to go home.

"Let me get this straight. She's so scared about going home that she comes on to you, a guy she met for the first time that morning."

John opened his mouth to respond, but this time I interrupted. "That's not a question," I said.

"She was so scared that she was willing to put out in exchange for a place to stay."

I shook my head.

"That is your theory, isn't it?" Hernandez said to John.

"He's asking you to speculate," I told John. "If you know why she was putting out, you can answer the question. If you don't, say so. Don't speculate."

"I don't know," John said.

Hernandez said, "You know, this woman was an accountant. I would have expected her to go to a hotel, she needed a place to stay. She could have afforded it."

"So we're done here?" I said. "You don't have any more questions?"

"Another thing that bothers me," Hernandez said. "She's scared to go in her apartment in daylight with you right there, then in the middle of the night she's okay with it."

I stood up. "Okay, then."

Jordan waved his hand at me. "Sit down, Counselor. I've got a question. Mr. Parker, did she say anything that suggested a reason why she didn't want to stay at your place any longer?"

John looked at me, and I nodded. "You can tell them what she said."

"I don't remember what she said exactly, but it was clear she thought we'd been followed to my place."

"Because a dog barked?" Hernandez said.

"She seemed to think it was barking at something, that someone was out there."

"You see anyone?"

"No."

"Hear anything other than the dog barking?"

"No."

The question and answer continued, Hernandez and Jordan now asking actual questions: When exactly did they leave John's apartment? Did they go straight to Wendy's or did they make a stop on the way?

"We stopped off to get my car, which was still in the parking garage downtown."

"Where was that exactly?"

John told them. He told how long the drive had taken from his place to the parking garage and from the parking garage to Wendy's apartment. He told about parking on the street, then going upstairs with her to check behind the shower curtain, check the wardrobe, look under the bed.

"I thought that would be it, but then suddenly she didn't want me to leave."

"'John, don't leave me. I want you so much,'" Hernandez said in falsetto.

John looked at me, then back at Hernandez. He didn't respond.

Jordan said, "What did she say? Exactly."

"She asked if I wanted to stay."

"And what did you say?" Jordan asked.

"I needed to get home and get some rest. I was starting a trial the next morning."

"A trial. Still going on?"

"It never started. The case settled."

"How long you stay at her place?"

"Maybe an hour."

"And that's where you had sex? Her place?"

John hadn't admitted to sex, but since he'd left a DNA calling card, there seemed little point in objecting. I turned over my hand, palm up.

"Yes," John said.

"Something you hadn't done at your apartment," Jordan said.

"No."

"What time did you leave her?"

"Just before eleven o'clock."

"A minute before? Five minutes before?"

"Say five minutes."

"Why didn't you spend the night?"

"She fell asleep. I…" John shrugged.

Hernandez said, "You'd got what you came for."

"The way she'd been acting was freaking me out."

"But not so much you didn't want to have sex with her."

"That's not a question," I said, keeping my eyes on the tip of my pen. My ears felt hot.

"She couldn't have been acting all that freaky once she was asleep," Jordan said.

"Still not a question," I said. I glanced up.

Jordan and Hernandez were looking at John. John was looking back.

"Let's go back to when you got to her place," Jordan said. "Did you see anyone around?"

"No."

Hernandez said, "What was she wearing when you left her? Bra and panties?"

John's eyes started to cut toward me, then stopped. "Probably not that much," he said.

Jordan said, "If she'd dressed to receive a visitor after you left, it seems like she would have put more on."

John didn't say anything.

"Which means the visitor would have undressed her again for reasons of his own," Hernandez said. "Undressed her, or forced her to undress. I wonder if the M.E.'s going to tell us she had sex with more than one person."

"Is that it?" I said. "No more questions?"

Jordan and Hernandez exchanged glances. "I guess not," Jordan said finally. "Not right now."

"So we can go?"

"No."

"How can you charge him? You can't tie the telephone wire to him, and you haven't got a motive."

"We have opportunity," Jordan said.

"Not unless he was carrying a three-foot piece of telephone wire around in his pocket. Do you carry telephone wire in your pocket?"

"I'm not planning to strangle anyone," Jordan said.

"Now you've got him planning to kill her when he left his apartment. Again, what's the motive?"

"Maybe he found the wire at her place."

"Maybe it was a weapon of convenience," Hernandez said.

"Any evidence of that? A kitchen drawer with pliers and screws and bits of wire, and John's thumbprint on the inside of it?"

They didn't say anything.

"If you can't tie John to that telephone wire, you haven't got squat," I said.

Jordan said, "We've got him inside her apartment as late as eleven p.m. The coroner says she died sometime between ten o'clock and midnight."

Hernandez said, "We've got pick-up sex right there in that time period."

"And the key to her apartment was on his dresser," Jordan said

That stopped me. Wendy's apartment had been locked up tight when I broke into it, and there had been no signs that anyone else had forced entry.

"She was asleep," John said, "and the lock on the door is a double-keyed deadbolt. There was a key hanging on a nail at the head of the stairs. I had to use it to get out, then to lock the door behind me. I wasn't going to leave her there with the door unlocked."

"Of course not," Hernandez said. "You're a gentleman."

Wendy's key ring had been in her purse, I thought. If, after John left, she woke up to let her murderer in, how had the murderer locked up after himself?

John said, "Why would I have bothered to lock up if she were already dead?"

"Somebody did," Hernandez said. "Delay discovery of the body, maybe."

"Keeping the key gave him an excuse to see her

again," I said. "That would explain him locking up after himself, even if he wasn't a gentleman."

John looked at me, then dropped his gaze.

Jordan said, "The killer has a key. The locked, double-keyed deadbolt tells us that. Your client's is the only one we've found so far."

"And there was only one nail in the wall to hang a key on," Hernandez added. "No reason to suppose more than one spare key ever existed."

Chapter 21

They fingerprinted John Parker, strip-searched him, and photographed him. He was still in his own clothes when they took him before the magistrate, a thin woman of about fifty who had an office there in the police station.

James Jordan had drafted and signed the complaint. He read it aloud.

John pleaded not guilty.

The magistrate set bail at 250,000 dollars.

"That's excessive, Your Honor," I said, and she looked at me over the narrow lenses of her glasses.

"Do tell," she said.

I told. "The accused is an associate attorney at a law firm here in Richmond. He's lived here since he got out of law school. His apartment is here, his friends are here, he's not a flight risk. And there's no way he can come up with a quarter-million dollars. Bail is supposed to be high enough to guarantee his appearance, not so high as to preclude the possibility of his making it altogether."

"He's accused of a capital crime. I could have denied bail altogether." She was talking about it in the past tense, as something already done.

Though I knew I had lost, I said, "You've as good as done that."

"When someone faces death by lethal injection, there may not be a lot of overlap between what he can pay and what it will take to guarantee his appearance."

I bit my lip, because she had a point.

"This is bad," I said to John when we were alone again. Jordan and Hernandez were off doing paperwork and getting John the orange jumpsuit he'd be wearing while he awaited trial.

"Do tell."

He looked depressed, but was evidently not too depressed to be a wise-ass. I said, "I'll talk to a bondsman this afternoon. I think I've heard that if you can put down ten percent..."

"I can't put down ten percent."

"You don't have twenty-five thousand dollars? Not even in your 401(k)?"

"Well, sure, in my 401(k)."

"You'll have to borrow against it. I'll get the forms you need and drop back by to get your signature."

"Larsen's going to fire me when he finds out about this," John said.

"No, he won't. Why would he?" I protested automatically. Then I pictured Larsen's face at seeing a secretary in the break room, at seeing me with a foot on my desk. "It would look bad to abandon you in your time of need," I said. "He'll wait until you're acquitted."

"Thanks for the encouragement."

"You've just been charged with capital murder. I don't have a lot to work with here."

There wasn't much left for me to do. Jordan and Hernandez came and got John. I said good-bye and left. I parked my car in the parking garage attached to our office building, and, before I went up to my office, stopped off at one of the shops in the food court for a bite to eat.

I got a raspberry tea and a deli sandwich and sat at one of the tables next to the black monoliths with the falling water. When I'd finished about half my sandwich, I began to feel better. It had not been a good week. It had been a terrible week—friend's murder, finding the body, attacks on me, boyfriend's infidelity, ex-boyfriend's arrest...When I'd sat down to eat, I'd been depressed almost to the point of being nonfunctional. Now, with a little food in my belly, I found my spirits rising.

Monday he cheats on me, I thought. By Friday he's in jail. "Who said there's no such thing as justice?" I mumbled with my mouth full of sandwich.

"Excuse me," said a voice at my elbow.

I threw myself forward across the table, tilting it and knocking over my tea as I spun out of my chair and landed on my keister, my bare legs splayed out in front of me on the marble floor.

The man in the blue apron had taken a step back. There were a couple of stains on the apron, and I recognized him as somebody I'd seen before bussing tables. He was about forty, with a thin face and very little chin. He looked terrified.

I held up a hand for help in getting to my feet, but he shrank back, his hands in front of him. "I'm sorry," he said. "I'm sorry."

"It's all right," I said. "It's my fault. I'm just a little jumpy."

I got awkwardly to my feet. It's not as easy as you'd think when you're wearing heels and a tight skirt that's trying to ride up on you, but I managed it. I brushed myself off and sat back down, noticing that several men and a couple of women—in fact, all those in the immediate vicinity—were looking at me.

Grimacing, I nodded around at them, making eye contact with this one and that one until everybody's attention had returned to his or her own business. "I'm sorry," I said to the busboy, who was still hovering a pace or two away from me. "I really am. I don't know why I reacted that way."

He nodded, his Adam's apple wobbling in his neck.

"Can I help you?"

He opened his mouth, but wasn't immediately able to get his words out. "The other day," he began, "the day when you and that other lady were here?"

I nodded encouragement.

"The other day when you and that other lady were here, you dropped something. I mean, I don't know if you dropped it, I didn't see you, but it was on the floor under the table when you left."

My gaze went to his outstretched hand. It was holding a CD jewel case with a picture of Taylor Swift on the front.

Chapter 22

The compact disc contained Excel files — spreadsheets. I opened one to take a look. A lot of my hopes were connected to that spreadsheet. I was anticipating some great revelation—but to me the file was nothing more than columns of numbers. I clicked print and opened another file. This one was clearly some kind of financial statement. I clicked print and opened another.

Take a look at these, and we'll talk, Wendy had said, but she was giving me way too much credit. I could tell a balance sheet from an income statement, but that was about the limit of my accounting abilities. What I needed was Wendy standing over my shoulder to tell me what I was looking at.

"What're you working on?" a voice said behind me, and I spun in my chair. Because the chair swiveled, the results were not as spectacular as they had been down in the food court. I stayed in my seat, though I found myself looking up at Pete Larsen through round eyes with my breath coming hard.

"Sorry," he said. "I didn't mean to startle you." He came in and sat across from me. "I left you a message this morning, but hadn't heard back from you."

My eyes shifted to the telephone and back to his spare, angular face. "I forgot."

He smiled. "What are you working on so intently?" He nodded at the computer screen behind me.

"Financial statements," I said inadequately.

His eyebrows rose.

"The Ledbetter case," I said, feeling both uneasy and pleased with myself at how easily the lie came to me. "Punitive damages are an issue, you know, and…"

He waved it off. "What I wanted to talk to you about is McCormack Labs," he said. "I have some good news."

I don't think he could have surprised me more if he'd sprouted horns.

"Good news?" I repeated.

"They've hired us to defend them in their class-action litigation, the mass-tort stuff."

To surprise me any more he'd have had to sprout wings as well as horns and fly around the room. He raised his fists in the air and shook them. "We've hit the mother lode, Robin," he said, his voice trembling. "In two years, the Northcutt law firm will be twice the size it is now. The partners' incomes are going to double."

I, of course, wasn't a partner.

"It means you, too, Robin. In a year, you'll be up for partner, and being a partner is going to mean a lot more at the Northcutt firm than it used to."

My smile was as sincere as I could make it. "That's great, Pete. It's really great."

"You're one of the first to know. I'll be meeting with Al Baldridge this afternoon to hash out the broad outlines of the deal. All goes well, and we'll be making a general announcement to attorneys and staff on Monday morning."

"Who's…"

"Al's the head of their legal department."

"Don't they have about sixty lawyers working for them? Why aren't they handling their litigation in-house?"

"They're transactional lawyers. They hammer out deals and draw up contracts. They don't have any experience in the courtroom."

I nodded. I had one more question, but I wasn't going to ask it. I'd had a message from Pete before eleven o'clock, and, when I hadn't responded, he'd come and found me. Why was he so anxious to tell me about this?

Pete's smile dimmed a bit, which was a relief, because it let me drop mine. "There is one thing," he said.

I braced myself.

"I understand a friend of yours worked for McCormack Labs, and she was murdered several days ago. I'm sorry."

Sorry wasn't one of the things Pete did best, but he was making an effort. I nodded.

"Al said he had one concern about taking us on. You."

"I was the concern?"

"He thinks you may blame McCormack for what happened to your friend. He said you might have some kind of bee in your bonnet."

"He said that? Bee in my bonnet?"

Pete's mouth twisted. "His words, I assure you."

"What did you say?"

"I told him Northcutt lawyers didn't wear bonnets and that you were a litigator, not a beekeeper. Was I right?"

I nodded, though not quite willingly. "Did it seem to satisfy him?"

"Yes, it did." Pete slapped his thighs and stood up. "Just so we're clear on that."

"Pete?"

He turned back in the doorway.

"How well do you know Al Baldridge?"

He shrugged. "I've known him slightly for years. I think we played a round of golf once upon a time."

"How many conversations have you had with him about us working for McCormack?"

"Two." Pete came back into the office and stopped directly in front of my desk, frowning down at me.

"Both of them this week?"

"Yes. Why?"

I shook my head, shrugged, and smiled, all at the same time. "I don't know. It all just seems kind of sudden, like it fell out of the sky."

He relaxed. "It's all tentative at this stage. Al and several members of his staff will be meeting with us over the next month or so, finalizing the agreement."

I sat back in my chair. "Sure."

He looked at me a moment, then turned to go. In the doorway he stopped. "I know this sounds crazy," he said, turning around again. "But I need your assurance you aren't going to mess this up for us."

"You have it."

He grinned. "Oh, I know. It's just that Al seemed

kind of…" His head moved as he searched for the right word. "…focused on you."

"Huh," I said. I remembered what Wendy had told me: *If what I've found are two sets of books, then the fraud goes all the way to the top.*

Chapter 23

Later that afternoon I ran errands, my first stop being a bail bondsman named Ricky "The Clubfooted Tornado" Anderson. It seemed that in earlier life he had been a professional wrestler. There was a poster on the wall behind his desk of a man in a red cape that I could only assume was Ricky Anderson himself—though the man on the picture looked nothing like the bearded, barrel-bellied, bald-as-a-goose-egg man on the other side of the big oak desk.

He had a lot of questions about John Parker, as well as a two-page form for me to fill out. Many of his questions had to do with John's family, and I was embarrassed to find that I couldn't answer many of them. After all, I'd been dating the man for nine months. Though I hadn't told him about my father's betrayal until this week—a raw wound, even after all this time—he'd heard more about my deceased grandma than I knew about his entire clan. His mother had been married a few times, I knew. She was in Houston, but I was uncertain as to what her current name was. Her first name, I thought, was Sarah.

"Sarah," Ricky, the club-footed tornado, repeated in a gravelly voice as he wrote the name on the back of the form I had filled out so sketchily.

"Or Linda," I said.

He crossed out Sarah.

"John has a sister up in Indianapolis."

"And her name?" He looked over his half-glasses at me.

"Maybe her name is Sarah."

"Sarah Parker?"

I nodded uncertainly.

"Her middle name wouldn't be Jessica, would it?" One corner of his mouth rose.

"Maybe I should take the form and get him to fill it out," I said.

He pushed it toward me across the oak desktop. "Maybe you should."

"But you can handle the bond," I said, seeking reassurance.

"If he deposits twenty-five thousand dollars with me, it shouldn't be a problem."

"Does he get any of it back?"

"Some of it. Maybe." He pointed at the papers in front of me. "That yellow sheet is our fee schedule."

"Thank you."

I'd gotten a form from the law firm's office manager that would allow John to borrow against the funds in his 401(k), so I was ready to return to the jail. I left my car in front of the bail bondsman's office and walked. It was only two blocks. As I walked, I reflected that the lack of genuine love in my relationship with John hadn't been all on his side. If I'd been more interested in him as a person, I'd know more about his family. I'd know more about a lot of things.

"You're a superficial person, Robin Starling," I said to myself. There were people on the sidewalk, but nobody reacted to my outburst. With the growing popularity of Bluetooth, it looked like half the people you saw were talking to themselves.

What concerned me was this: If I hadn't loved John, even after nine months, then maybe I wasn't capable of love.

"That would suck," I said as an approaching group of women in nursing smocks parted to walk around me.

None of them even glanced at me.

John's mood seemed to have deteriorated since that morning. I thought at first that the seriousness of his situation had been working on him, but it turned out to be cellmate problems.

"The guy they've got me with is in a Lewis Carroll play with the Richmond Community Theater. He gets out of jail the week before opening night, and he keeps wanting me to read his lines with him. He talks all the time. And his breath smells of sour vomit."

"Not like the sweet vomit you're used to?"

He made a face.

"What's the name of the play?" I asked. "I didn't think Lewis Carroll was a playwright."

"What difference does it make? 'Through the Looking Glass' or something. I don't know."

"What's he in for, your roommate?"

"Unpaid parking tickets. He gets a hundred dollar credit for every twelve hours he spends in jail."

"And they put him in with an accused murderer?"

"He thinks it's cool."

"I think it's irresponsible."

"He's a two-hundred-pound biker who likes to sit around in his underwear so I can admire his tattoos. If anyone's at risk, it's me."

"So he likes you."

"Yeah. Great." John started filling out forms and signing things. It was a half-hour before he finished.

"It's the weekend," I said. "Even if they're willing to wire this into your checking account, it'll be Monday before we can get you out of here."

He nodded. "O frabjous day," he said. "Callooh. Callay."

"Have you called the office?" I asked. "What have you told them?"

"That I'm sick."

"That's it? Sick?"

"Specifically that I'm blowing chow at both ends."

"Not quite as poetic as 'callooh, callay.'"

"Oh, I didn't put it quite that way. I said just enough to suggest the details are something nobody wants to hear."

Chapter 24

It was nearly six o'clock when I turned onto my home street, which was earlier than usual. I had work piling up in my inbox, but I wanted to get into my house and out again well before dark. I stopped at the curb in front and walked across the street to Dr. McDermott's.

On my way out of downtown, I had called him on my cell phone, and his door opened as I came up the sidewalk.

"You ready?" I asked.

"I'm ready." He sounded a little grim, though, and, unlike that morning, this time he was holding a pistol. He pulled back the slide as he came down the steps to the sidewalk, and it slapped back into place.

"You bought a gun," I said.

"I already had it. After what happened to you last night, I took it out and cleaned it."

I tried to think back fifty years to what war he might have been in, and the closest I could come was Korea. "Were you in the Army?" I asked. "Or..."

"Army, but this came later. No good reason for getting it, I guess. When I was an intern, several of us bought guns and took up target shooting." We turned onto my sidewalk. "You're welcome to stay with me, you know."

"I know, and I appreciate it. But I have a friend who's out of his apartment for the next couple of days, and that'll be fine." The friend, of course, was John Parker. It would be Monday or Tuesday before I could get him out of jail, and I had a key to his place.

"But you…" He fell silent as I stepped up onto the porch and put my key in the lock. I think we were both holding our breaths as I pushed open the door.

I don't know what we expected. The door swung slowly inward to reveal my living room—no visible intruders, everything looking just as it had the last time I'd seen it.

I exhaled. Dr. McDermott did the same.

"I think we're okay," I said.

He nodded. When I went into the house, though, he stayed close behind me, and he kept his gun up, pointed at the ceiling like a cop on television.

In my bedroom the light on the answering machine was blinking lazily. One message. I sat on the bed and pressed the button.

"Robin. I—" A woman's voice, sounding hesitant. "If you get this, call me." She gave a number and hung up.

"Who was that?" Dr. McDermott asked me.

I shook my head.

"If you get this? She's calling your house. Why wouldn't you get it?"

"I don't know."

"I don't like it."

I didn't like it either, but that just made it par for the course. I wrote the number down on the square notepad by the phone and ripped off the top sheet. "I'll call her when I get where I'm going."

We were out of the house in fifteen minutes. I said good-bye to Dr. McDermott on the front lawn, got in my car, and watched him cross the street to his house. Then I pulled away from the curb and drove to John's apartment.

After I had moved in, laying out my toilet articles on the bathroom counter, hanging up some clothes and stacking others along the bedroom wall in neat piles, generally making the place my own, I was feeling hungry. John had a frozen brick of lasagna in his freezer, a case of beer in his refrigerator, and an open bag of chips in one cabinet, but almost nothing else.

What the heck, I thought, turning on the oven to 450. I tried to screw the cap off a bottle of Corona, though I wasn't a beer drinker. The cap hurt my hand and didn't come off. There was a bottle opener stuck magnetically to the side of the fridge, though. When I'd got the cap off, I took a swig of the beer and choked on it, then noticed a lime sitting alone on the counter by the sink. It couldn't hurt.

With half the lime squeezed into the bottle and a slice of lime wedged into the neck, I tried again and found that it didn't help, either. But I carried the bottle into the living room where John's phone was, so I could make a call while the oven preheated.

"Hello?"

It was the woman from the answering machine, but I still couldn't place her.

"This is Robin Starling," I said.

There was a silence. "Are you all right?" she said at last. "I heard…"

I waited.

"I heard you were attacked."

"Who is this?"

"Oh. Brooke Marshall."

The network administrator for McCormack Labs, the one who'd run away from me in the food court at Regency Square Mall. I took another drink from the bottle, grimaced, and said, "I was attacked. Cord around the neck, just like Wendy Walters."

"I'm sorry."

"You didn't do it."

"Do you know who did?"

"Unh unh," I said. "Do you?"

Again the silence. Finally she said, "When I got back from lunch yesterday, I was pretty upset. I made kind of a big deal at the office about all the questions you'd been asking. Then today people were talking about it."

"About…"

"About you being attacked."

It was my turn not to say anything.

"I wasn't able to discover how they knew about it," she said. "There was nothing in the paper, nothing on the internet. I checked."

"Who was talking about it?"

"Pretty much everybody. I don't know who started it."

"What did they say?"

"The first I heard about it, one of the data entry people said, 'Hey, Brooke, you know that woman you were talking about yesterday? Somebody broke into her house last night and tried to kill her.'"

"What data entry person?"

"A woman named Cheryl, but she'd just heard it

162

from someone else—another clerk, I think."

I swallowed another mouthful of beer, by this time hardly noticing the taste. "What did she hear exactly?"

"Just that someone had broken in and tried to kill you."

"Did she hear how he tried to kill me?"

"No. She had the idea he hadn't succeeded, but she didn't have any details. What was stirring everyone up, I think, was that we'd just been talking about you yesterday. Or I'd been talking about you. And there'd been a lot of speculation as to what you were after."

When she hung up, I drained my beer in a few long swallows and went back into the kitchen for another. The oven dinged, indicating it had reached 450. I put in the lasagna.

Did people kill people over accounting irregularities? I asked myself as I squeezed a wedge of lime into another Corona. Wendy had stumbled onto something she wasn't supposed to know, and she had gone outside the company with it. Wendy was dead. Then I'd known something I wasn't supposed to know, or, more accurately, I'd looked as if I did. I wasn't dead, but someone sure wanted me that way. And John Parker was in jail, doing dramatic readings with a tattooed perpetrator of moving violations. John, of course, had never known anything; he'd just let his libido get away from him.

My beer spiked with lime juice, I went back into the living room and redialed Brooke's number. She answered with the same cautious hello, and I said, "If I emailed some files to you, could you take a look at them?"

"What kind of files?"

"Excel."

"I guess so."

"They're what Wendy gave me when she came to see me on Monday."

I could hear her breathing.

"Okay," she said finally. "Send them on."

"What's your email address?"

She gave it to me. While the lasagna cooked, I turned on John's computer, put in the CD, and sent Brooke an email with copies of the files attached. Then I went back into the kitchen for a third beer. For something that tasted like it might be cow urine, it was surprisingly addictive.

Chapter 25

The next morning I had German pancakes at the IHOP on West Broad Street, then drove back to John's place. It had been a long time since I'd found myself at loose ends on a Saturday, but there I was. Last Saturday, I'd had a boyfriend; today he was in jail. Last Saturday, I'd had a home that required regular attention. Today I was dispossessed and hanging out at John's.

Despite the reversals of fortune, my spirits were high as I parked my car and walked down the sidewalk toward John's building. The air was crisp; the sky was clear; I had the day to spend as I pleased...Somehow, it was enough.

I turned the corner and stopped, because there was a girl in jeans and a T-shirt sitting on the steps. She stood, dusting off her fanny with the palms of her hands, and I recognized her by her thick mop of red hair. It was Brooke Marshall.

"What are you doing here?" I asked.

"You didn't answer your phone."

"How did you..." I stopped. I had called her from John's apartment, of course, so if she had Caller ID, she had the number.

"I used a reverse directory on the web to get the address," Brooke said.

I nodded.

"I'd assumed you were calling from home. I called there first and left a message."

We climbed the stairs to John's apartment, and I asked if she wanted a beer. "I don't drink myself," I said, as I got a couple of bottles out of the fridge. "Or I didn't. Actually, I guess I started last night." I held out a bottle to her.

"It's nine-thirty in the morning," she said as she took it.

I popped the top off my own bottle. "Is your point that we're getting a late start, or an early one?"

She gave me a funny look, which I'm sure I deserved. Nonetheless, she took the bottle opener from me, opened her beer, and took a swallow.

"Just put it on the coffee table," I said, referring to the bottle cap.

"It's been bothering me that I left a message," she said. "I may have been too…"

"Explicit?"

She nodded. "Do you mind if we go by your house and erase it?"

I shook my head. "Consider me your partner in paranoia."

"What will we do with these?"

"Have a seat," I said. "We'll have to finish them first."

It was just a few minutes after ten when we drove by my house. I didn't even slow down. Brooke, who had been following the street numbers, swiveled in her seat. "Wasn't that it?" she said.

"That was it."

"What—"

"We're scoping it out first." I turned at the corner and came back down the alley.

My garage door was closed, and the short driveway was empty. All was as it should be. I drove on past.

"Are we just going to keep circling?"

"For a while." And we did. I went out a block and circled, out another block and circled again. We passed a few parked cars, some in driveways, some on the street, nobody in any of them. I turned toward home.

"Do you know what kind of car your attacker was driving?" Brooke asked.

"Nope. I have a stalker named Eddie Unger who drives a Caprice Classic, but I don't see it either."

She was sitting with her back against the door, studying me. "That's not a joke, is it? You're serious about the stalker."

I flashed her a grin. "I'm afraid so." I turned into the alley and from there into my own driveway. "Eddie's not dangerous, though, or I don't think he is. He fell in love with me when he put his arms around me and I smashed his nose with my forehead."

"That sounds like a story."

"I'll tell you about it over lunch. Last night wasn't the first time this week I've been attacked."

The garage door rumbled upward.

"When was the first time?"

"Monday. The day Wendy gave me her disc."

We went in. Everything was the way I had left it, but the answering machine didn't show any messages.

"Are you sure you left one?" I asked. "Maybe you made a mistake."

"I didn't."

I flipped open the compartment that housed the tape—I'd tried digital once, but hadn't liked the sound quality—and saw that the tiny cassette was gone. Someone had been in my house that morning, and whoever it was had taken my message cassette.

Fingers were digging into my arm. I looked around into Brooke's big eyes.

"What message did you leave exactly?" I asked.

She shook her head. "I said I'd looked at the files, and it looked bad. I think I said somebody was going to jail."

"So they know we've got Wendy's files."

"Let's get out of here," she said.

I nodded.

Back at John's apartment, we went straight to the refrigerator. This time Brooke didn't quibble. She took the bottle from me, opened it with the bottle opener, and started glugging.

When she lowered the bottle, a third of its contents were gone.

"It's not even eleven," I said, watching her over the misting mouth of my own Corona.

"That's why I'm saving the rest of the bottle for my next swallow."

I laughed. "You're a wild thing, Brooke Marshall."

In the living room, I took the easy chair, and Brooke sprawled on the sofa, clutching the neck of her bottle in a two-fingered grip.

"You realize you can't go home," I said.

"I can't go to work either."

"No. You're here for the duration."

We sipped our beers in silence for several minutes before I asked, "When you said it looked bad, the files, what did you mean?"

"There are definitely two sets of books there. They both purport to cover the same time period, but each has all kinds of entries that aren't reflected in the other."

"Can you tell which set is the real one?"

"One set matches the documents on file with the SEC. I checked their website this morning."

"So that would be the phony set."

"I would assume so."

I nodded. After a few more swallows of beer, I said, "Where is your computer?"

"My car."

"I was just thinking. Somebody has been in my house today. Now that they've listened to that message, they've probably been in yours."

Her eyes widened a bit.

"You're safe enough here," I said, but she shook her head.

"No, I don't think I am."

"How—" I stopped. "You have caller ID, and you didn't erase it. There would have been no reason to."

"No. And I'm not the only one who can use a reverse directory."

I took a big breath and let it out, then swung my leg off the arm of the chair. "We've got to move," I said.

Chapter 26

I drove my Beetle, and she followed in her own car. She didn't want to go home even to pick up a change of clothes, so we went to Target to get a few things. After picking up some toiletries, a few changes of underwear, a couple of shirts, a pair of pants, and a cute green dress that looked great with her red hair, we went looking for a hotel. We passed three hotels before I pulled into a Courtyard not far from the IHOP where I'd had breakfast. Finding us would not be a matter of contacting the nearest hotel.

When we'd parked and locked our cars, Brooke asked, "How are we going to pay for this? Do you have cash?"

"Thirty or forty dollars. Not much."

"If we use a credit card, we'll have to use our own names. They'll find us in half-a-dozen phone calls. Actually, the hotel's probably going to want a credit card on file regardless."

I opened my purse and took out John's wallet, which he'd given me for safekeeping when they'd booked him. "Allow me to introduce myself," I said. "Mrs. John Parker."

"You're married? Who—"

"John Parker is my erstwhile boyfriend."

"Cool."

We got a room with two queen-size beds. It had a minibar, too. Soon Brooke and I were sitting cross-legged on the beds with candy and cracker wrappers on the covers around us, a little bottle of Jack Daniels, an empty soda can, and an open can of Heineken on the nightstand.

"It's not the usual kind of thing," Brooke said.

We were talking, not about what seemed to be our incipient drinking problem, but about the two sets of accounting records.

"What do you mean?" I asked.

"Usually, in the scandals I studied in business school, the company's trying to hide debt and inflate revenue. Enron, WorldCom, Sunbeam—that's what all of them were trying to do."

"That's what Wendy made this sound like."

"Well, there's some of that. Mostly, though, McCormack seems to be hiding revenue—disguising it, anyway."

My head was getting a little fuzzy, and it occurred to me that I might be overdoing the booze and sugar thing. "Why would anybody want to hide revenue?" I said. "I thought that's what drove the stock price."

"It is." She nodded significantly, but in my alcohol-addled state I didn't see the significance.

"So no one would want to hide revenue," I said.

"Not without a compelling reason."

"A compelling reason like..."

"The revenue isn't revenue they can report."

"But—" I stopped. I was getting a glimmer here. "Al Capone didn't report his income from whiskey smuggling," I said.

"An ounce dealer doesn't list what he pays for his cocaine on Schedule C as his cost-of-goods-sold," she said. "He pays no taxes, which is great, but there are worse things than taxes."

"If he tries to pay cash for a car...," I said.

"Or tries to deposit it in the bank, or if he lives visibly beyond his means..."

"Then the feds get him for tax evasion."

"Just like they got Al Capone," Brooke said.

I got up and went to the minibar for another bottle of something—I thought I'd try a white wine. As I crouched in front of the open door of the little refrigerator, I looked up at her. "So what are you saying?" I asked her. "They're hiding revenue?"

Brooke giggled. "You're looped."

I opened my mouth to protest, but what came out was a bark of laughter. It set Brooke off. She laughed until tears were streaming down her face, and I laughed with her.

We both stopped abruptly when I snorted a wad of snot onto the carpet. We looked at it, shocked, then our eyes met, and we started laughing again.

Eventually, the mirth subsided, having worn us both out. I was lying on the floor on my back, and Brooke was sprawled on the bed.

"What I'm saying," Brooke began, a little breathlessly.

"Money laundering," I said.

"Exactly. McCormack has money that isn't reflected in its official set of accounting records. It's got to be dirty money, or they wouldn't hide it. Wherever it comes from, they put it into McCormack or one of its subsidiaries, and they report as much of it as they think they can without arousing suspicion. The rest stays hidden until they sell an asset or something that will allow them to show a gain."

I thought about it. "Can you tell where the money's coming from?"

"Nope. Just that it's there."

"And you only know that much because Wendy stumbled across the real set of books."

"Uh huh."

"I don't guess there's any way to know where she stumbled across it," I said.

"No."

"Do you think it's drug money?"

"Isn't it always?"

I was silent, having never devoted much attention to the hows and whys of money laundering.

"What do we do now?" Brooke asked.

I thought about it, or started to. Perhaps Brooke thought about it, too, but she was still asleep when I woke up, still on the floor, my muscles stiff and my head aching slightly. It was dark outside, and the digital clock on the nightstand glowed 10:35 through the bottles and cans that were clustered around it.

I went into the bathroom to brush my teeth and splash water on my face. As I dried my face with a hand towel, I walked back into the bedroom. Brooke's face was mashed against the bed, her wild hair hiding most of her face, and her mouth sagging open. She grunted, and I laughed. One of her eyes opened.

"What are you looking at?" she said in a fuzzy voice.

I gave her a bright smile and went back into the bathroom to hang up my towel.

"Oh!" Brooke exclaimed, a bit too loudly.

She was sitting up on the bed. "Remind me never to do that again," she said.

"Advil?"

She nodded, her fingers against her forehead.

I got it out, filled a glass with tap water, and chased down a couple of pills. Then I filled another glass and took it to Brooke with the bottle of Advil.

She went into the bathroom and came out about five minutes later, her face looking freshly scrubbed.

"Want to go out for a bite?" I suggested.

She looked momentarily doubtful. "Okay," she said.

About twenty minutes later, we were busy putting ourselves around a couple of half-pound burgers, going at it like we hadn't eaten all day. I went back over everything that had happened since Wendy showed up in my office, making sure Brooke knew everything I did.

"We're going to have to do something, you know," Brooke said when she'd finished her burger and slowed down a bit on the fries.

"I know." I nodded vigorously, still chewing. "We go on eating and drinking like this, they'll have to get a horse trailer to haul us around."

"I meant about McCormack."

"I know."

"Though the gluttony is going to kill us."

"And the drinking."

"I think that's just part of the sin of gluttony."

"Sin?" I hadn't been thinking in terms of sin, but then, my parents had stopped hauling us to church before I was a teenager. Having finished my burger, I took the lid off my Coke and glugged it. "I was thinking of it as a little self-indulgence."

"I'm pretty sure it's a sin."

"Well, thank you, Your Holiness." I wiped my mouth on the back of my wrist. "What's the definition of sin, anyway?"

Her eyes shifted, and she didn't answer, which I took as an I-don't-know. We seemed to have plumbed the depths of our combined theological knowledge.

"How about McCormack?" I said. "Any ideas about it?"

She slurped thoughtfully at her Dr. Pepper. "No. Not any."

"Me either."

I sat back with one leg on the seat, my arm on the seat-back and my soft drink held loosely in one hand.

Brooke said, "There's nothing we can do, not by ourselves. We're going to have to talk to somebody."

"Okay. Who? Marty Nolen?"

"Not Marty Nolen."

"And not Al Baldridge, your general counsel. You can't have two sets of books without somebody in top management being in on it, and he's a pretty good candidate."

"Because he tried to buy you off through your law firm," Brooke said.

"Sure, but anybody and everybody right up to the CEO himself could be in on it."

"So we have to go outside the company."

"Can we be certain none of the auditors are involved?"

She thought about it. "No."

"That's what Wendy thought. What have we got on this CD? Is it obviously a second set of books?"

"Yes," she said.

"Obvious to an outsider? I have to tell you, I opened them up, and all I saw were Excel files filled with columns of numbers. The rows and columns had little one-word labels that didn't mean anything to me, and some of them weren't labeled at all."

Brooke didn't answer.

"How about an outside member of the board of directors?" I suggested. "If we can find one in Richmond, great. If we can't, we fly to New York or Atlanta or wherever we have to. All we need is the disc and maybe a little corroborating evidence."

She pushed back her plate. "Corroborating evidence?"

I grinned. "Sounds funny, doesn't it? You have to be able to say it three times real fast before they'll let you out of law school."

"What kind of corroborating evidence?"

"A witness, preferably. What would be really nice is to turn somebody at McCormack, somebody who's in on the money laundering or the accounting fraud."

"Okay. And barring that?"

"Don't give up so easily. We just keep putting the pressure on somebody until he cracks."

"And who's going to mount this campaign of terror?" she asked. "You and me? Aren't we the ones who are afraid to go home?"

It did sound like a fantasy. "Documentary evidence then," I said. "Maybe we could turn up a memo somewhere."

"Note to file: instructed accounting to handle the following transactions off-book…"

"An email," I said.

She shook her head. "Security at McCormack is

incredible. After thirty days, all email goes through the digital equivalent of a paper shredder. Of course, a recent email might help us, if we can get to it."

We sat for a while looking at each other, neither speaking.

"So what do you think we should do?" Brooke said at last.

"Me? I came up with the campaign of terror, the smoking memo, and the incriminating email."

"Neither the memo nor the email is likely to exist."

"Then we're back to the campaign of terror," I said.

Chapter 27

We looked up Al Baldridge in the phone book, along with Marty Nolen and Peter Lawrence, the CEO himself. Lawrence lived in the west end on the north bank of the James River. Baldridge lived in Windsor Farms. Martin Nolen lived in Mechanicsville, a northern suburb of Richmond. We pinpointed the addresses on Google Maps.

"What now?" I said.

She shrugged. "It's midnight."

"I'm not sleepy."

"Neither am I."

"Want to go for a ride?"

Peter Lawrence's house was closest, almost straight down Parham from where we were. It actually looked less like a house than a museum, set on a vast, rolling lawn that went all the way down to the river.

"He does all right for himself," Brook said. The house was big and square and built of stone blocks that were bigger than my dresser. There was grillwork around all hundred-and-two of the windows.

"I guess he's never had you over," I said.

"Huh."

There were cars on the curving drive, lights in the downstairs windows. With my car window down, I thought I could make out the faint sound of music.

"What are the chances that Al Baldridge is at that party?" Brooke said.

"I don't know. Greater than zero, though it's late and I wouldn't count on him being there long." I put the car in gear again and rolled forward.

We took Cary Street to Windsor Farms, an exclusive neighborhood laid out on circular and diagonal streets rather than the usual grid. Al Baldridge lived in a three-story house with dormer windows and a slate roof. It was big, but it wasn't a museum—just a big house with a well-manicured lawn that probably cost no more than a million five. Though the porch light was on, all the windows were dark.

"What do you think?" Brooke said.

"I don't know." I opened the car door and got out.

Brooke opened her own door. "Where are you going?"

"I'm going to check out the garage."

I felt exposed, but I strode down the driveway as if I owned the place. The garage, detached from the rest of the house, was part of a converted carriage house with an upstairs apartment. Both of the single-car doors were solid wood, but there was a window on the right side of the garage. It was darker inside than it was outside, but I thought I could make out the outlines of a car in the space closest to me.

"What do you see?"

I lurched upward, nearly choking on my tongue. The voice belonged to Brooke, who evidently had padded up the driveway right behind me.

"Don't do that," I said.

"You didn't think I was going to wait in the car."

I took a breath. "I think there's a car in there. I can't tell for certain."

"I don't think anybody's home. There're no lights at all."

"It's late," I said. "They're probably asleep."

"Or at a party at the CEO's house."

"And you think Al's wife is with him? What about the kids?"

"Maybe there aren't any kids."

"Maybe there isn't any wife," I said.

"Exactly."

I put my head back to look up at the house. It didn't look as if anybody were home.

"Okay, let's try it," I said.

"Try what?" She followed me as I walked around to the front of the house, mounted the steps to the front door, and rang the doorbell.

"What do you think you're doing?" she whispered fiercely. "It's the middle of the night."

The chimes sounded inside the house, followed by silence. "Casing the joint. At least they don't have a dog," I said.

"I'd bet on an alarm system, though."

"The birthday of his firstborn," I said.

"What?"

"If we could get in, we could punch that into the keypad to deactivate the system."

"We don't even know if he has a firstborn."

"If he's on wife number two, it could be her birthday," I said.

"Or their anniversary."

"I think we don't know enough about Al Baldridge."

"No kidding," Brooke said.

We retreated.

I started the car, but didn't turn on the headlights. After a moment, I killed the engine.

"We're going to wait for them to come back?" Brooke asked me.

"I'm thinking," I said. "When we get back to the hotel, you can get on your computer. Find out everything there is to know about Al Baldridge."

"I can access payroll records to get his social security number. Once I've got that…"

"Excellent," I said.

A car was approaching. I let my seat back to avoid being silhouetted by the headlights, and beside me Brooke did the same. The car's clock showed 1:04.

The car began to turn and, as the headlights left my car, I lifted my head in time to see it finish the turn into Baldridge's driveway. From the car's profile, it looked like a Jaguar.

It disappeared behind the house, and I started my own car and rolled backward to keep it in sight.

The garage door on the left was rumbling upward. The Jag rolled in, and its brake lights flared and went out. A man got out on the driver's side, and a woman got out opposite him. They weren't very close to us, but in the available light I would have placed him at about fifty and his wife at thirty.

"Trophy wife," Brooke said softly.

"We need to find out how long they've been married and whether there are kids."

"You still thinking about alarm codes?"

"Heck, I don't know," I said. "I'm just thinking."

We drove out to Nolen's house next. It was in a new development with large homes, most of them close to three thousand square feet, with spotlights set in the ground to highlight the landscaping. An umbrella visible over top of Nolen's privacy fence suggested he had a pool.

"Nice," Brooke said.

"What do you know about his family?"

"He's divorced and remarried. I think number-two already had a boy who would be seven or so now. He has a couple of girls from his first marriage, but they don't live with him."

On the far right of the house, a light was visible through tall windows with plantation blinds. There weren't any cars in the driveway, but with a three-car garage there wouldn't be. We had to assume somebody was home.

I put the car in gear and pulled away from the curb. "How do you know all this about his family?" I asked.

"The divorce happened since I've been at McCormack, maybe three or four years ago."

"The remarriage?"

"About six months after that."

"So maybe he was cheating with number-two before the first one said bye-bye."

"What difference does that make?"

"If he cheated with number two, he'd cheat on her."

"So?"

"Maybe she knows it."

"So?" Brooke was beginning to sound exasperated.

"I was thinking about our campaign of terror.

Callers who hang up when the wife answers…"

"Caller ID," Brooke objected.

"We block it. A pair of panties under his car seat. Help me out. I'm reaching here."

We went back to the hotel. It was the middle of the night, but neither of us was sleepy yet. Brooke logged onto the hotel's wireless and started surfing. I watched her awhile, then fished out the Gideon's Bible from the nightstand. I thought I'd look up gluttony and maybe lust, which seemed to be the particular brands of self-indulgence I was most prone to. The Bible had no index, though. I glanced up.

"Who are you on?" I asked.

"Baldridge."

"So you think he's the one to start with?"

She grunted, her lower lip between her teeth.

"We know he's in on it," I mused, "because he's the one hiring the Northcutt law firm to shut me up."

"Suppose the CEO just told him to hire you?"

"Okay, either Baldridge or Peter Lawrence is in on it. Martin Nolen would have to know about it, too, don't you think?"

"I'll work on him next," she said, her fingers tap-dancing on the computer keys. "Baldridge first."

I turned my attention back to the Bible. About two-thirds the way through there was a lot of stuff in red, which I knew from childhood Sunday School classes were the words of Jesus. The first passage I focused on read, "If anyone desires to come after me, let him deny himself, and take up his cross daily, and follow me. For whoever desires to save his life will lose it, but whoever loses his life for my sake will save it." Not a lot of room for self-indulgence there, I thought.

I flipped pages, reading a passage here and there. Jesus was quite the storyteller. The word *commandment* caught my eye: "This is my commandment, that you love one another as I have loved you. Greater love has no one than this, than to lay down one's life for his friends." I looked up. Though the line was vaguely reminiscent of Sydney Carton in *A Tale of Two Cities*, I was thinking about John Parker. Had I ever loved him? I'd enjoyed him, certainly, but that didn't seem to come close to the greater love Jesus was describing. On the other hand, this greater love was way beyond my aspirations. When it came to laying down one's life, I preferred a walk in the park.

I said, "Are we still thinking about breaking into Baldridge's house?"

She looked up briefly. "It was your idea," she said. "Campaign of terror."

"I guess we could smear things on the wall." I closed the Bible and put it back in its drawer. The Book of Mormon was in there, too, but I knew less about it than I did about the Bible, so I left it alone. After several minutes, I said, "It would be nice if Mr. Baldridge had a stack of incriminating documents lying on the desk in his study."

"Sure."

"If he has incriminating documents, though, it seems more likely they'd be at McCormack."

She looked up again. "Trust me. We don't want to break into McCormack." She looked back at her screen, thought for a few seconds, then moved her finger on the touch pad and clicked.

"How about this?" I said. "We enter the house, we

find his computer, we take it with us. We'll be in the house ten minutes, tops, and you'll have a ton of information to dissect at your leisure."

"It's a plan," she said. Her mind was obviously on what she was doing, though, and I wasn't sure she meant it.

Late the next morning, Sunday, we had breakfast at a Denny's near the hotel. I read somewhere that the Grand Slam breakfast has about a thousand calories—seriously—but I managed to eat all of mine, eggs, pancakes, bacon, sausage, and all.

"I'm developing some really bad habits," I told Brooke as the waitress topped off my mug of coffee. I could hardly claim to be denying myself daily.

"Tell me about it," Brooke said around a mouthful of food.

"If we don't wrap this up soon, I'm going to waddle when I run."

Brooke nodded, swallowing. "Tell me about it."

"I think you're a bad influence." I slurped my coffee.

"I was going to say the same thing about you."

The previous evening, I'd fallen asleep before she finished with the computer, which evidently didn't happen until sometime after three a.m. She'd discovered a lot. Al Baldridge had been married to his current wife, the former Anita Hoeffer, for four years. He'd acquired the house in Windsor Farms at roughly the same time as his new wife. He had two children by a prior marriage: Justin, age nineteen, currently a student at Mr. Jefferson's university in Charlottesville, and Mandy, still in high school somewhere. Brooke had been unable to find out where.

"I'd guess she lives with her mother, but I couldn't find her," Brooke said.

"I'm surprised you found out as much as you did."

"I had help, but I had to spend fifty dollars of your boyfriend's money to get it."

I waved a hand. "Cheap at the price."

"I put the credit card back in your purse."

"Good, then John can pay for breakfast, too." I felt a pang when I said it, though. Maybe Bible-reading was bad for your peace of mind.

Brooke had full names, birthdays, and anniversaries. From those, we could develop a list of numbers that might—or might not—include the alarm code we needed, assuming we needed one at all. Justin's birthday was at the top of the list. Anita's birthday was next, followed by the anniversary of the second marriage—incredibly, the same as the anniversary of the first.

"Al Baldridge is a man of habit," I commented.

"We're going to do it then? When?"

"Tonight."

"Suppose he's at home? How likely is it he has social commitments two nights in a row?"

"Then we'll go plant some panties on Marty Nolen," I said.

Chapter 28

That afternoon, just after four, we stopped the car two doors down from Al Baldridge's house and on the other side of the street. From our vantage point, we could see both the end of the driveway and the front door of the house.

"All right?" I asked as I killed the motor.

"Except we don't know if they're in there."

I pulled out my cell phone. "We will in a minute."

An answering machine picked up.

"No one home," I said.

"You mean no one's answering."

"Well, yes. 'No one home' is my conclusion."

"Suppose they're just not answering?"

"Why wouldn't they answer?"

"They could be having sex?"

"They've been married four years. They're not going to be having sex in the middle of the afternoon."

"Even if they're not home, it's only four o'clock," Brooke said. "They can't be out for the evening. They could be back anytime."

"Okay, you win. We wait." I settled back in my seat.

The day was hot and humid—in Virginia, most summer days are hot and humid—and, without the air conditioner going, I could already feel sweat beginning to form on my face. The open windows kept us from dying of heat stroke, but they didn't do much for comfort.

After five minutes or so, Brooke said, "I'll go ring the doorbell."

A bead of sweat ran down my back between my shoulder blades. "I'll go with you."

We both got out of the car.

"What are we going to say if they answer the door?" Brooke asked as we started up the sidewalk.

"We'll deal with that when we have to."

I mounted the steps to the porch and pressed the doorbell. We waited, then Brooke pressed the doorbell. Nothing happened. Brooke looked at me, and I nodded. We headed for the back of the house.

The upper part of the side door consisted of twelve panes of glass. We looked through them into the kitchen. We were at the back corner of the house, and a chimney largely shielded us from the street.

"You got the list?" I asked, and Brooke held up the hotel pad with its column of numbers. I plucked from my pocket the surgical gloves we'd picked up at Walgreens and worked them onto my hands. Brooke, tucking the pad under her arm, took out her own gloves and did likewise.

One of my T-shirts dangled from the back pocket of my jeans. I pulled it out and held it so that it hung down over the pane of glass closest to the doorknob. "You do the honors."

Brooke put out a gloved hand to hold the T-shirt in place.

I gave her a look. Then I took a breath, shifted position, and swung my elbow.

The crack of the glass sounded like a rifle shot, and fragments tinkled on the kitchen's tile floor. Brooke lost her grip on the T-shirt, and it fell to the ground. Several jagged blades of glass still hung in the frame. I pried out a couple of the larger fragments and tossed them on the ground. Then I reached in to turn the thumb latch and then the doorknob.

That's all it took. We were inside. No alarm sounded, and there was no alarm pad on the wall.

"By the front door," Brooke said, and we banged through a swinging door into a hallway and raced for the front of the house.

There was no alarm pad inside the front door either. Evidently, Al Baldridge didn't have a security system.

"That's a relief," Brooke said.

I nodded, my heart still hammering, my gaze wandering upward. An enormous chandelier, large enough to flatten us, hung from a ceiling two stories above us. There were stairs at both ends of the entrance hall, going up, and an upstairs hallway overlooked us.

"The bedroom?" I said, no longer believing there was an alarm system, but wanting to be thorough.

Brooke nodded. I went up the stairs at one end of the entrance hall; Brooke went up the stairs at the other. We arrived at opposite ends of the upstairs hallway that ran the width of the house. On one side of the hall was the stained-wood balustrade and, beyond it, the chandelier. On the other side were doors interspersed with a half-dozen painted portraits in large, ornate frames. I opened the first door I came to; at the other end of the hall Brooke opened another.

"Bedroom," she called.

I was looking at one, too. I guessed by its size and its uncluttered appearance that it was a guest room. It had a bath opening off it and a sliding door that was probably a closet. For what we were looking for, it seemed like the least promising room in the house. I closed the door and continued down the hall to the set of double doors, which were in the center of the house.

Brooke got there ahead of me and pushed open the right-hand door into the master bedroom.

"No alarm pad here, either," I noted, scanning the walls.

Brooke walked around the king-sized bed. "Good thing," she said. "I wasted a lot of time searching through the private life of Al Baldridge, though."

"Not necessarily. You never know what will come in handy," I said. The master bedroom was a big one and had a row of windows overlooking the backyard. A Stairmaster stood in one corner. An open door on one wall revealed a large bathroom with flowered wallpaper and a couple of pink, fluffy throw rugs. The two closed doors opened on large walk-in closets. On the wall opposite the bed hung a big, flat-panel TV.

"Nothing up here," I observed. "No computer, no briefcase."

Brooke bounced across the bed toward the door. "You check the closets for a file box or something, maybe tucked against the wall under the hanging clothes. I'll go down and see if there's a study."

She left the room, not quite running. I hesitated a moment, then went to the nearest closet.

It was Anita's. Two rows of clothes hung on one side, one above the other. Her dresses hung from a single rod opposite them. On the wall at the end of the closet were built-in drawers. I peered under the hanging clothes, opened and closed the drawers, then flipped off the light and went to the other closet.

It was his. Dark suits and dress shirts, all of them white; a tie rack; a shelf with more men's shoes than I'd ever seen in one place outside of a shoe store. I was crouching to look under the suits and dress shirts when from downstairs I heard what sounded like the front door whooshing open. My heart lurched in my chest. I hoped to heck it was Brooke, but couldn't imagine why she'd be messing with the front door. I moved toward the bedroom door, which she'd left standing open about a foot, and stopped when the entrance hall came into view.

A dark haired woman in her early thirties was in the foyer. I caught just a glimpse of her before she moved out of my field of vision. I moved away from the bedroom door, my heart hammering. Even if Anita went into the back part of the house, I had no way to track her movements and was unlikely to escape unseen. I didn't know where Brooke was.

I heard footsteps on the staircase and glanced through the open door again to see Mrs. Anita Baldridge, if that's who she was, coming up. I retreated deeper into the bedroom, my eyes darting to the closet doors, to the bathroom, to the big bed. I was trapped. The bed's side rails were too close to the ground for me to slide under them. The footboard was a little higher, perhaps high enough to allow me to scoot under the bed from the foot, but perhaps not. There wasn't time to try it and be wrong.

I hesitated between the master bath and Al's closet for only an instant before hotfooting it into the bathroom. Almost immediately I regretted my decision. In Al's closet I might have been able to push my way in behind the suits and shirts. In the bathroom, there was nowhere to hide: Even the shower had a clear plastic door. But there was no time to go back.

I got an idea. It was a pretty awful idea, but when you have only one you can't be too picky about it. After only a moment's indecision, I stepped out of my shoes and unsnapped my jeans. I pushed my pants down to my ankles and stepped out of them, then shrugged out of my T-shirt. The bedroom door opened with a faint creak, and I went still.

My gaze shifted, and I caught sight of myself in the mirror. My bra and panties matched for once, both a deep maroon. I ran my hand back through my hair to give it a little more body, noticed the surgical gloves, decided I didn't have time to take them off. They were nearly flesh colored anyway, and with luck Anita wouldn't notice.

I turned and headed for the bedroom, my pulse beating wildly in my neck.

"Al?" I said as I pulled open the bathroom door and stepped out. "Al, did you…"

I'd surprised Anita in the act of tossing her purse onto the bed. She froze with a sharp intake of breath. Her eyes locked on mine for an endless second, then cut downward. She herself was wearing black slacks and a blouse that, coincidentally, almost matched my underwear.

"You're not Al," I said.

"Who..." She couldn't get it out.

"Anita?" I opened my eyes as wide as I could get them. "Oh, my God." I put a hand over my crotch and an arm across my breasts as I backed toward the bathroom.

"You're kidding me," Anita said, her voice rising. "You've got to be freakin' kidding me."

"I'm sorry," I said to her. "I am so sorry."

Downstairs, the front door slammed. Anita snatched up her purse, and I stepped back into the bathroom and closed the door before she could throw it at me—but the bedroom door banged open as she went out into the hall. Already I was shrugging into my T-shirt.

I picked up my jeans and left the bathroom in time to see the bedroom door still vibrating inward. From the balcony Anita screeched something at her husband below. I had one leg in my jeans, and I hopped sideways in an effort to get a glimpse of what was going on.

Anita was still on the balcony, and she had a voice on her. I couldn't get much sense out of what she was saying, except that she was punctuating it heavily with profanity. Below was a man with a reddish scalp and thinning blond hair—the unfortunate Al, I imagined. He tried to break into Anita's tirade, but all I could catch was the bewildered tone of his voice.

Anita wasn't having any. She moved along the railing, and, in the foyer below, Al moved with her, still trying to calm her down. I heard "Anita" and "honey," but I don't think she did. She clunked furiously down the stairs, and he met her at the bottom, his hands outstretched.

"Anita, calm down. What's in our bedroom?"

She hit him with her purse about six times, and Al stumbled against a small glass table covered with framed photographs and nearly took it down. Anita jerked open the front door and went out. The table delayed Al enough that by the time he got to the door and got it open, a little Miata convertible was reversing down the driveway. At the end of it, the suspension squealed and gears clashed. Anita, I imagined, was gone.

Al looked up then, and he saw me. I stepped away from the door, but the damage was done. I heard an angry exclamation and, immediately, footsteps on the stairs.

My eyes darted about for some avenue of escape, but I'd explored the possibilities before and come up empty. The bedroom door banged open, and he was there in the doorway, breathing hard. "Who the hell are you?" he said.

I straightened. "I'm a friend of Wendy Walters."

"Who?"

"You know who."

"What about Wendy Walters?" His eyes were moving, making sure, perhaps, that I was alone, or looking for a weapon to use against me.

"McCormack Labs has been keeping two sets of accounting records," I said. "Wendy discovered them, and within twenty-four hours she was murdered."

He took a step toward me, and I stepped back.

"What do you know about it?" I asked him.

He stepped sideways, and I took another step away from him before I realized he was maneuvering me into the corner.

"Are you the one who ordered her killed?" I asked.

194

"I wouldn't order anyone killed." He was breathing heavily. "I'd do it myself." He was not an especially big man, about my height, but he had probably thirty or forty pounds on me. I couldn't afford for him to jam me into the corner.

"So you knew about the two sets of records," I said.

"I don't know…what you're talking about." He came at me. I tried to duck under his outstretched arms, but his swinging forearm caught me in the forehead and snapped my head back. Before I could recover my balance, he grabbed me and threw us both to the floor, landing on top of me with his arms around me, pinning my arms. He raised up on his elbows, and I tried to head-butt him, but my forehead did no more than graze his chin as he shifted his weight to free an arm. His punch to the side of my head half-stunned me, though he wasn't at an angle to put much force into it. I got my arm up on that side and managed to take part of the next punch on my forearm, twisting in a futile effort to scramble out from under him. I took another blow to the side of my skull and, my head ringing, pressed my forearm against the side of my head in a desperate effort to protect it. I couldn't get my other arm free. Al reared up, drawing his fist back to drive his next blow into my face.

Brooke wrapped both arms around his. "No!" she shouted, stepping back in an effort to pull him off me, but she lost her grip, and he fell against me. He waved his arm as Brooke came back at him, and the side of his head brushed my face. I felt a swirl of flesh-covered cartilage against my lips, and I tried to catch it in my teeth, but missed. I drew breath into my lungs and screamed.

Al jerked as if he'd been hit with a Taser and fell sideways, and I managed to scramble out from him on feet and elbows, before rolling onto my hands and knees, my arms trembling so violently that they could scarcely hold my weight.

"Are you all right?" Brooke's hand was on my back.

Al got his feet under him, but as he tried to rise, Brooke kicked at him, and he avoided the kick only by falling backward onto his butt.

"You can't get away with it," I said, my head turned toward him. "It always comes out."

"You're delusional," he said. He pushed to his feet, his back against the wall.

"The files say otherwise."

He began to move crablike toward the door, picking up a piece of rose quartz from the nightstand as he went. When he reached the door, he closed it and leaned against it. He was breathing heavily, his eyes moving.

I got to my feet, wishing I'd had time to get my shoes back on. "You do know what I'm talking about," I said.

"Which one of you is Robin Starling? It's you, isn't it?"

"I'm Robin Starling."

"You don't know when to quit, do you? You're one stupid, nosey bitch."

"I'm a bitch who'll quit when the job's done," I said.

His upper lip curled as he hefted the chunk of quartz, which was roughly the size of a fist. Suddenly,

I was terrified.

"What, you're going to throw rocks at us?" I said.

He looked from me to Brooke, as if deciding which of us to target.

"Why kill us?" I said. "Why not press charges on the burglary? Who's going to listen to us anyway?"

"Jared Thompson," Brooke said. My gaze flicked toward her.

"What?" I said.

"Jared Thompson, the fund manager for the Odyssey Healthcare Fund." Odyssey Investments occupied most of an office tower in downtown Richmond. "I don't know why I didn't think of him before. He'll understand the numbers."

Al lurched forward, and I dove at him, managing to hit his throwing arm as he let the chunk of quartz fly and catching him around the hips as I landed mostly on my knees in front of him. I heard a *thunk* from behind me and a yelp from Brooke as Al banged back against the door. He roared, sounding more like a wild animal than a middle-aged lawyer, and his knee jerked up, raking a breast and catching me under my chin. I fell back onto the floor, half dazed, but rolling in an effort to put some distance between us as Brooke charged past me.

That's where it all went south. Al backhanded Brooke into the wall, then stepped forward and stomped down on me, the heel of his shoe catching me at the hairline. I collapsed. Though I still struggled to get my hands and knees under me, I'd lost any sense of what I was doing and what the stakes were. A black fog had filled the room. I felt a hand on my neck. The bedroom door swung open, and I was propelled through it as unable to resist as if I were caught in a nightmare.

"No, no, no," I was saying as my socked feet slipped on the hardwood floor of the hall, as the railing high above the tiled floor of the front hall pressed into my waist. I folded over the rail, only half-conscious, but my hands closed on two of the balusters, and I pushed at them in an effort to keep from going over.

A woman screamed behind me, and Al's body slammed into me, pushing me off my feet and driving me headfirst over the rail. I lost my grip on one of the balusters as Al's bulk rushed downward, raking my body, leaving me hanging by one hand, my feet swinging in space. Above me, Brooke leaned over the rail, her hands outstretched, and I swung my free arm, reaching for her, but my grip on the single baluster had begun to slip. Brooke grabbed at my wrist and caught it, but it wasn't enough.

I lost my grip and fell.

Chapter 29

The floor of the second-floor hallway was maybe twelve feet above the tiled floor of the foyer, but I'd been hanging, the length of my body making up nearly half the distance. I fell about seven feet, landed on my socked feet, and spilled forward onto Al, who lay where he had fallen.

For perhaps half-a-minute I thought I had broken both feet on the hard tile, and I lay with my face mashed into Al's buttocks, my moans muffled.

Gradually the pain faded. Brooke was there, her hand on me, asking if I was all right.

I pushed up to sitting position, still gasping. "I'm fine," I managed. I poked at Al, but he didn't move.

"Al?" I got up and rolled him onto his side. Brooke cried out, perhaps because Al's crossed eyes were most macabre thing either of us had ever seen. I pushed my fingers into his neck, but if he had a pulse, I couldn't find it.

"Is he…"

I looked up from Al's fixed, cross-eyed stare.

"Should we…"

"Call the police?" I said. "We can't."

"It was self-defense."

"It was an accident."

"He tried to kill you," she said. "He tried to kill both of us."

"The kitchen window's broken, and we're wearing surgical gloves. You can't break into a man's home and then claim self-defense when he ends up dead."

Her hands went to her face. She lowered them. "Suicide?"

I shook my head. Anita had seen me in the bedroom no more than fifteen minutes ago.

"Right. Who kills himself by jumping off a second-floor balcony?" Her eyes widened. "I know. The people who killed Wendy."

"How are we going to sell that?"

"Hold on." Brooke disappeared into the back of the house.

I went upstairs to retrieve my shoes, still in the master bathroom, but stopped when I entered the bedroom and saw the chunk of rose quartz embedded in the sheetrock across from the door. Brooke had had a near miss.

I got my sneakers and sat on the bedroom floor to put them on. My eyes kept returning to that rose-colored rock, but my mind was on the predicament we were in. If Al's death was murder—and the police were never going to see it as anything else—then the two burglars in the house were the prime suspects. That suggested that the two burglars' first order of business was to get out. I got to my feet and went back downstairs where Al was still sprawled on his side, unmoving.

I found Brooke sitting at a bleached-wood desk in what looked like a study. A sheet of paper was sliding out of the printer. She picked it up and held it out. I took it.

It said, "Peter Lawrence is next."

"What's this?" I asked.

"Don't you see? He's the CEO. It ties the murder into what's going on at McCormack Labs."

"How does it do that?"

She pulled a flash drive from one of the ports on Al's computer. "I copied Wendy's files to his hard drive. If I can find a disc..."

"We gotta get out of here," I said, interrupting. Anita had seen me in the house, but, as bad as that was, getting caught in the house with her husband's corpse would be even worse.

"Okay, okay. I'll just leave the folder open on his computer." I hurried her out of the office. As we passed Al's body, she took the paper she'd handed me and stooped to put it on the floor next to his head.

Disaster had overtaken us. I thought I was handling it, but by the time we got to my car, I'd developed a bad case of the shakes.

"Can you drive?" I held out my hands so she could see the tremor.

Brooke frowned at me, nodded, then slipped into the driver's seat. After we'd put a couple of miles between us and Al's house, she pulled over to the curb.

"Okay," she said. "What's wrong with you? Is it that you almost died, or is it that Baldridge did die?"

"It's more practical than that. Al's wife was with him when he came in. You must have heard her."

"So?"

"So she saw me." I told Brooke the story.

"You...you stripped down to your underwear?"

Her voice went into the high treble range on the last word.

"I was trying to sell a story."

"And then she went down...she went down...and started beating Al...with her purse." She ended in a squeak. She laughed, then hiccupped, then started to cry. I slid as close to her as the gearshift would allow and put an arm around her. "It'll be all right," I said.

"How can you say that?"

"I'm a liar," I said. "Lawyer, I mean."

She started laughing again, her face still wet with tears, but she choked on her laughter and it ended in a fit of coughing. When it was over, she seemed better, though.

"Maybe I should drive," I said. "I'm all right now."

"Maybe you'd better."

We each got out of the car and walked around it to trade places.

I turned onto I-64, heading back toward the hotel, but almost immediately Brooke said, "Exit here."

"Here?"

"Parham Parkway."

I turned into the exit lane. "What are we doing?"

"We're going shopping."

"I don't get it."

"There's an outfit at Dillard's I've been looking at. We'll go straight to the rack, then find a sales clerk."

I gave her a puzzled look.

"It's your alibi, you dope. We've been shopping all afternoon. I was looking at the outfit when we first got to Regency Square. You finally talked me into it and we walked back down the mall to get it."

"We'll get a receipt with the date and time on it," I said.

"Right. The receipt will support my testimony."

"Your testimony. You'd lie for me?"

"I'm the one who pushed Al to his death, in case you've forgotten. We're in this together."

It was two minutes to six when we parked the car. We went in the Dillard's entrance, and Brooke found her outfit.

"It's cute," I said. "Are you going to try it on?"

"What for? I had it on not two hours ago." There was a sales clerk within earshot, and Brooke motioned to her.

"The exact same outfit?" I said.

"I think so. Anyway, it's the same size." She handed it across the counter to the sales clerk, whose nametag said Jamie, and Jamie rang it up. The total was 184.92.

"A hundred eighty-four dollars," I said.

"Yeah. I don't know why I let you talk me into it."

"It does look good on you."

I patted her butt, which drew a glance from Jamie. Brooke gave me a look, too, and I smiled affectionately at her. We wanted Jamie to remember us, and now I was pretty sure she would.

"Was it you who was helping us earlier?" I asked, frowning at Jamie as she handed back Brooke's charge card. "It seems like it was somebody named...I can't remember. Maybe it was you."

"It was probably Becca. People say we look a lot alike."

My face cleared. "That was it. Becca."

After Dillard's we stopped at The Coffee Cup for a couple of cups of French roast coffee. Brooke stirred in cream and three packets of Sweet-n-low, which kind of defeated the point of French roast, in my opinion.

I found myself yawning. "I'm so tired I can barely keep my eyes open," I said, sipping the strong, hot coffee. "Maybe it's reaction setting in."

"But we've done good, don't you think?"

I glanced at the tables around us. "We killed a man."

"I mean building an alibi. And with any luck the police are going to find those phony accounting records and start digging."

"Okay. Aside from killing a man, we've done well."

She didn't say anything for a while after that. "I guess you're right," she said, finally. "It's kind of a big thing, even if it was self-defense—and it was self-defense. We've got to keep telling ourselves that."

"It may help us sleep better," I said.

We finished our coffee, and I bussed our table, setting our mugs on the counter and dumping our trash, which included our receipt and a couple of napkins. The empty Sweet-n-low packets stuck to the tray, but I put the tray on the stack without bothering about them. I started to turn away, then stopped. There had been a receipt stuck to the tray below mine. Probably too recent to help with an alibi, but...

I lifted all but the bottom tray. No receipt was stuck to it, but when I raised the stack in my hands to peek under it, there it was—a receipt, stained yellow-brown with coffee, stuck to the bottom of the tray. I braced the stack of trays on the edge of the trashcan and peeled it off. The receipt had a time printed on it, 05:17, probably about the time that Al Baldridge was falling past me to his death. I observed that we'd had a Viennese cappuccino and a latte with vanilla syrup, and then I pushed the receipt into my jeans.

"What was that?" Brooke asked me as we walked away down the mall.

"More documentary evidence of how we spent our afternoon."

Chapter 30

Once again, Brooke and I spent the night at the Marriott. The next morning was Monday, and Brooke was up before me. When I came out of the bathroom, she was half-dressed and putting on makeup.

"Where are you going?" I asked.

"Same place you are."

"I'm going to work. I've got a client to get out of jail, for one thing."

"I'm going to work, too."

"My work?" I asked.

She gave me a look. "What would I do at your work?"

"You can't go to yours. We talked about that, remember?"

"I know, but Al Baldridge wasn't dead then. I've been thinking about it. Everyone's going to be talking about him. How's it going to look if I turn up missing at the same time the murder story breaks?"

"Nobody's going to associate him with you."

"My absence might cause somebody to start asking questions. I want to avoid any official inquiry as to where I've been and what I've been doing."

"When Anita Baldridge identifies me, you're going to have to confirm we spent Sunday afternoon at the mall," I said.

"And that will be more believable if everything else about me is normal."

She was probably right, but it was dangerous, I thought. Too dangerous. "Whoever took the tape off my answering machine knows you've been in contact with me, and they know we've got Wendy's files."

"Going to work is dangerous for both of us. Who knows what kind of accident they have planned for you as you leave the office today?"

It was an obvious thought, but I hadn't had it. A shiver ran down my spine.

"I'll be safe enough," Brooke said. "There'll be a lot of people around me—and I might even accomplish something."

"Like what?"

"I don't know. I might hear something."

I took a breath and exhaled it. "Okay," I said. "I'll drive you and see you into the building to make sure nobody waylays you in the parking lot. Is there a company cafeteria or somewhere you can eat lunch?"

"They always send out for sandwiches for anyone who wants one. I can eat mine in the break room. It's always pretty crowded. What time can you be there to pick me up?"

"I'll pick you up at five," I said. "Just come out with the crowd, and I'll be here."

Monday was the day I was supposed to get John out of jail. Once at the office, I called the custodian of his 401(k) and learned that the check had gone out and should arrive that morning with the FedEx delivery.

While I waited, I worked to get everything else off my desk so that when the check arrived I'd be free to act.

I was reading an opponent's brief, jotting notes on a legal pad, when I realized someone was watching me from my doorway. I looked up.

It was Police Detective James Jordan, his hands in his pockets, his shoulder propped against the jamb. He wore a tie and striped shirt, but no jacket.

"The police officer with two first names," I said.

He sighed, then came in and dropped into one of the client chairs.

"What are you doing here?" I asked. Beyond the glass walls of my terrarium, a couple of lawyers walked by, but they didn't even glance in my direction. "How did you get past the receptionist?"

"I flashed my badge, said I knew the way."

I waited.

"You think of McCormack Labs as the bad guys, don't you?" Jordan said.

"You mean, just because they keep breaking into my home and trying to kill me?"

"How many assaults have there been on you? Two?"

I nodded. "I'm not saying they assault me every time they break in. Sometimes they just snoop around and take stuff."

"What have you been doing about it?"

"Taking precautions."

"You've got a client to defend, too."

"John Parker? Yeah."

"Been working on it?"

"It's been the weekend."

"You spend it at home?"

"I haven't felt too safe at home."

"Where have you felt safe?"

"The Marriott out on West Broad Street."

"You staying there alone or with someone?"

"You jealous? I thought you were married." I looked pointedly at the ring on his left hand.

"I may have found copies of those files your friend Wendy gave you."

"You may have?"

"Mm hm."

I waited, but he didn't elaborate. "Look," I said. "I bill by the hour. Tell me what you want, or get out of here."

"I want you to come down to the station with me."

"Why? Something about John Parker?"

He shook his head.

"You're not doing a very good job of telling me what you want," I said.

"You don't know?"

By way of answer, I smiled at him and cocked my head.

"I'd like you to participate in a lineup," he said.

"A what? What for?"

Jordan grimaced and looked away from me. Then he turned back and met my eyes. "Al Baldridge was found dead in his home late last night."

My head went back. "I've heard that name. Isn't he general counsel for McCormack Labs?"

Jordan didn't respond, just sat evaluating my performance.

"He just hired our firm to do McCormack's trial work," I said.

"I hope you got it in writing."

I frowned. "You said 'found dead.' Do you mean…"

"We're treating it as a homicide. Will you do the lineup?"

"Heck, no. Who have you got who wants to take a look at me?"

"What are you scared of?"

"Plenty. Let's say you've got someone who claims he saw a tall young woman coming out of Baldridge's house yesterday. You get a wild hare, and you show him my picture. He says maybe, he can't tell. Then you put me in a lineup. Maybe I'm the tallest young woman there, but in any case I'm going to look pretty familiar to him, right? He's been studying my picture. Then once he's identified me, I've got hell to pay."

"Where were you yesterday?" Jordan asked.

"What time yesterday?"

"Let's just start from the time you woke up. You said you spent the night at a hotel?"

"I'm not going to give you my itinerary, even if I can remember it. Do you have probable cause, or don't you? If you do, I don't have any choice about the lineup. Arrest me, and we'll get it over with."

He sat there awhile without saying anything. Then he slapped his thighs and stood up. "Okay," he said.

I wasn't sure what he meant by that, so I stayed in my seat, looking up at him. He went to the door, turned back, and said, "I like you, Robin, I really do."

I smiled, but not like I meant it. After he left, I didn't move for about five minutes. Then I exhaled noisily, deflating like an inflatable doll right there in my chair.

The check from John's 401(k), made out to Ricky Anderson, the bail bondsman, arrived by FedEx at about 10:30. I tore open the big envelope, studied the check for a few seconds, and kissed it. John was out of jail, at least temporarily. I took the elevator down and crossed the lobby to the parking garage, only to find James Jordan sitting on my car.

I stopped dead, but it was too late to retreat. He had already seen me.

"Are you stalking me?" I said.

His mouth stretched. "As you pointed out, I'm married." He lifted his foot from the bumper and stood up. "I was about to give up on you."

"Do I sit on your car?" I said. "You're going to scratch the paint. What are you doing here anyway?"

He pulled a folded paper from the inside pocket of his jacket. I took it from him and flapped it open. It was a warrant for my arrest.

He took it back from me and jerked his head. "Let's walk," he said. "Ray's got the car parked in the next block."

We were out on the sidewalk before I thought of anything to say. It was turning out to be another hot day. I had a briefcase in one hand and a purse over my shoulder, not having thought to leave either one in my car. In a block, I was going to be sweating.

"Why wait for me in the parking garage?" I asked Jordan. "Why not just come in and get me?"

He shrugged. "After my visit, I thought maybe you'd be heading out anyway. And I didn't want to embarrass you, in case this does turn out to be a wild hare."

"Your witness identified my picture, I take it."

"It was a tentative identification."

"So you want to do the lineup."

"That's still the plan."

I shivered suddenly, despite the heat. "Even though I'm going to look familiar to this guy just based on the picture you showed him."

"It wasn't that good a picture. I got it off your firm's website."

I knew that picture. It made me look like a giraffe.

"I hope you have some tall women in the lineup."

When he didn't say anything, I repeated it. "I hope you have some tall women…"

"I know. I hope so, too."

Great, I thought. An unmarked Crown Victoria pulled up beside us, Ray Hernandez behind the wheel.

The police station was at least air-conditioned. We took the elevator up to the second floor, walked down a long, tiled hallway, then turned a corner. "In here," Jordan said.

I went in, and he closed the door behind me. There were a handful of women in the room, only one of them in uniform. That woman was on her feet. The other four were women within five years or so of my age, all of them various shades of blonde. Everyone was sitting down, so it was just a guess that a couple of them might be within a couple of inches of my height.

"You Robin Starling?" the woman in uniform asked.

"That would be me."

"Have a seat. It shouldn't be more than a few minutes."

I sat in a plastic chair next to one of the taller women, putting my purse and my briefcase against the wall. The dress I was wearing a cotton-blend, so I had something to wipe my sweating palms on.

"You nervous?" asked the girl beside me. She had the cheekbones and the flawless skin of a fashion model.

I nodded, but didn't say anything.

"I was nervous my first time in a lineup."

I raised my eyebrows.

"My name's Laura. I'm one of the administrative assistants in the homicide division."

"Robin Starling," I said.

She nodded. "The suspect du jour."

There was a buzz, and the cop picked up the phone. "Okay," she said, replacing it in the cradle. "Everybody line up."

I stood fourth in a line of five, Laura just behind me. The cop gave each of us a white piece of card stock. I glanced at mine. On one side was a large number 4; on the other, the words, "You're not Al. Anita. Oh, my God. I'm sorry. I'm so sorry." My own words. A chill rippled through me just as the inside door opened on a narrow room.

I took a breath and exhaled it. We started forward, shuffling to keep from running into each other. We stopped.

"Turn right," a man's voice said.

We turned. I think I was expecting a large plate of dark glass, but it was actually a long mirror. I found myself holding in my stomach and trying not to squint.

"Turn to the right."

We turned. I was trying to comfort myself with thoughts of my cooked-up alibi, but without much success. Even if a good lawyer could use it to create reasonable doubt, it was going to be a long, expensive struggle.

"Face forward again."

We faced forward. I was conscious of sweat beaded on my forehead.

"Number one. Step forward and read the card."

Number one stepped forward and read it in a flat monotone.

"Thank you. Number two, step forward and read the card."

When my turn came, I stepped forward and read the card in the same flat monotone the others had used. Laura, coming after me, was the only one to put any expression in her voice.

"Thank you, that's all."

The lights went down a notch, and we filed out. In the waiting room, everyone was sitting down again, so I took the chair next to Laura.

"How long does this part last?" I asked her.

"Not long. Ten, fifteen minutes." She crossed her legs. I crossed mine, too.

It was twenty minutes before Jordan opened the door. "Okay," he said. "You can go now. Thanks."

The female cop took one of the women by the arm as they filed out. The others seemed free to go where they would. Jordan jerked his head and fell into step beside me as we clacked down the hall.

"So what happens now?" I asked.

"To you? Nothing. The witness identified my secretary."

"Laura?"

"You know her?"

"We just met."

We got to the elevators, and he pushed a button.

"We don't look anything alike, you know," I said.

"That's not true. You're both tall, athletic..."

"She's a knock-out."

"...attractive."

"Pulease," I said. "I'm not in her league."

He glanced at me.

I said, "If your witness picked out Laura, then whoever he saw leaving that house doesn't look any more like me than you do."

Jordan eyed me speculatively as we continued to wait for the elevator.

"What?" I said.

"The woman at the Baldridge house was in her underwear."

"That would make a heck of a lineup. You might get Victoria's Secret to sponsor it."

One of the elevators opened. As we got into it, he said, "Well, I said it was a wild hare."

"I thought I was the one who said wild hare."

"Whoever."

"So does Laura go to jail now?"

"What?"

"If your witness had identified me, I'd be going to jail, wouldn't I? What was Laura doing at the Baldridge house in her underwear? Inquiring minds want to know."

"You're a piece of work," Jordan said.

Chapter 31

Ricky Anderson's office was only a couple of blocks away from the police station. A bell tinkled as I went in, and Anderson's secretary looked up from her desk.

"I'm here to see the Club-Footed Tornado," I said. "Is he in?"

He appeared in the doorway of the inner office, filling most of it. "Robin Starling," he rumbled in his deep voice.

"That's me."

We went back, and I gave him the check and the paperwork John had filled out.

"How long is this going to take?" I asked.

"Couple of hours. I'll give you a call."

I picked up a sandwich on my way back to the office. I'd barely finished eating it when one of the junior partners latched onto me to help him with some last minute revisions to a brief he was working on. It was a pain, but it did keep my mind occupied until Ricky Anderson's call came a little after four.

"Ms. Starling?" Anderson said. "We're outside the jail, standing together on the front steps. Would you like to speak to him?"

"Please." I waited a moment. "John?"

"I'm here. Are you coming to get me?" He sounded tired.

"I'm on my way."

Rush hour had already started. It took fifteen minutes to get my car and get across downtown to him. John was in his own clothes, but they were rumpled and he had a couple days' growth of beard. Ricky Anderson, the Club-Footed Tornado, had done his work and gone.

I pulled up in front of John and leaned across the front seat to push open the passenger door.

He grinned at me, though it looked like an effort. "Boy, do you look good," he said as he dropped into the seat.

"Don't get too enthusiastic. I'm not what's for dinner."

He pulled the door shut. We were on the Downtown Expressway when he said, "What is for dinner?"

"Your choice—but we've got to pick up somebody first."

"Pick up somebody?"

I told him about Brooke. "We've been staying at the Marriott. It isn't safe for either of us to go home."

"You could have stayed at my place. You still have a key, don't you?"

I wobbled my head. "I've got your set, too, from when they arrested you, but your apartment may not be safe either." Which took a little more explaining. "We'll be at the Marriott again tonight. There're two beds. Maybe you ought to join us."

His eyes cut toward me. "What does this Brooke look like?"

"Like peaches and cream, if that makes any difference. I'm offering basic shelter here. You're going to have to keep your appetites under control."

It was a few minutes after five when we pulled into the McCormack parking lot, going against the flow of the departing employees. I pulled into an empty space and called Brooke's cell phone, but all I got was her voicemail. When I tried the number for accounting, I got seven rings and a recorded message.

"I don't like this," I said.

John raised his eyebrows. "Is something wrong?"

My watch said a quarter past five, and the parking lot was nearly empty. "Let's go," I said, pushing open the car door and swinging my legs out.

"Go where?"

"We're going in after her. Come on."

John opened his mouth as if he were going to protest, but he shut it again without saying anything. I have to say it: I like a man who knows when to keep his mouth shut. He got out of the car on his side.

I led the way to the door of the second building on the right. It was a heavy metal door, painted a dull red, with a narrow pane of reinforced glass above the knob. For a moment I was afraid it would be locked, but the knob turned and the door gave when I pushed it.

It opened on a long hallway with industrial-grade carpeting and a suspended ceiling. We walked along it, John slightly behind me, passing a couple of closed, unmarked doors, then an open door that revealed a small room with a copier and a wall of white cabinets.

As I slowed down to check it out, John asked, "Do you know where you're going?"

"Not a clue."

I led on, and the hall opened into a large room divided into cubicles. Along the edge of the room were offices, mostly closed. Again I hesitated. Brooke had never mentioned whether she had an office or a cubicle.

I heard a raised voice, a man's, and I moved swiftly in the direction it came from. Halfway around the cubicles, I stopped, waiting, and, when the voice spoke again, I pinpointed the office. The door was closed, but the nameplate said *Martin Nolen.*

A woman spoke, her words indecipherable and her voice unrecognizable, then the man spoke again. I pressed my ear to the door.

"Not a chance," he said.

"You can't hold me here." The woman sounded like Brooke, but I wasn't sure.

"I can't? You leave now, there won't be a job for you in the morning."

"Then I won't have a job in the morning." After a moment, "Get out of the way, Marty."

The man laughed, and it wasn't a pleasant laugh.

A hand seized the top of my shoulder, pinching painfully, and, as I turned, another hand closed on my throat.

It was a tall man with short-cropped, black hair and a week's growth of beard. I recognized him: He was the man who had walked into the parking garage with me the day Wendy had come to see me. My eyes rolled in search of help as he lifted me onto my toes, but John seemed to have disappeared.

I croaked something unintelligible, even to me,

and then I saw John. Instead of doing something helpful, like launching a full-scale attack, he put a hand on the man's shoulder and said, "Hey, what the hell do you think…"

The man kept his grip on my neck, but he let go of my shoulder to drive stiffened fingers into John's solar plexus. John staggered back, his mouth open and his wide eyes filled with panic as he struggled to draw a breath. When the man had let go of my shoulder, I managed to take a step back and take some of the pressure off my throat. I kicked at the man's knee. Unfortunately, in my half-inch heels I teetered enough that I missed his kneecap, and I was so close to him that there wasn't a lot of force in my kick anyway. I lost one of my pumps, and he stepped into me. His hand tightened again on my throat.

John blundered into him from behind, and the man lost his grip on me. He turned on John and hit him twice. I planted my bare foot and drove the pointed toe of my remaining dress pump up into the man's buttocks, kicking with enough force to rip the seam in the side of my dress.

"This is ridiculous," a voice shouted from behind the closed door. "Who in the…" The office door was jerked open from the inside.

My kick was a miracle kick, the toe of my shoe evidently driving right into the unprotected center of the circle of pelvic bones. I hit the bullseye. The man lurched forward, then fell onto his hands and knees, leaving John hunched against the wall with blood running down his face. I kicked again, this time catching the man between his legs, my instep smashing up into more unprotected parts and driving him forward onto his face.

As he curled onto his side with a catlike mewl, one hand to his groin, a man came out of the office. Brooke spilled past him into the hall as he grabbed at me, and John, though still stumbling and off-balance, stomped vindictively on the head of the man on the floor.

I stepped back to avoid the grab, losing my remaining shoe in the process.

"You!" said the man who'd grabbed at me, who'd come out of Martin Nolen's office.

It was my first look at Nolen, assuming that's who he was. He was built along the lines of a tree stump, shorter than me by several inches, with a big, wide head, heavy shoulders, and short, thick arms.

"How come you to recognize me, Marty Nolen?" I said. "Unless you're into criminal assault and murder, there's no reason you should know who I am."

"You're fired," Nolen said, jabbing a finger at Brooke. He pointed at John. "I don't know who the hell you are. And you—" He turned to me. "You are going down." He charged, not what I'd expected from the head of accounting, and his shoulder caught me in the chest and drove me into the wall with such force that I hit the back of my head. John, fortunately, chose that moment to reenter the fray. He leaped on Nolen's back, first one arm and then the other slipping beneath each of Nolen's arms. Nolen staggered under John's weight, but didn't go down. John had him in a full nelson, forcing his head down, and Nolen, his short arms sticking almost straight out, slammed backward into the wall. The sheetrock split, and John's right arm lost its hold.

I curled back my toes and drove the ball of my bare foot into Nolen's knee. *Kick like a girl* is often used as a term of denigration, but, I tell you, it should be a term of approbation. Nolen's leg collapsed, and he fell sideways, taking John with him to the floor even as I fell back against the wall. John lost his grip, and Nolen tried to scramble into sitting position, but he was emitting short, desperate moans and clutching at his knee. Brooke interrupted his efforts with a kick of her own that caught him in the side of the head and slewed him around to put him on his face.

"We've got to get out of here," she said. "They're completely desperate."

"You're telling me," I said. I bent to pick up one of the shoes I'd lost, and the man who was not Marty Nolen groaned suddenly and rolled onto his back.

"Ha!" Brooke shouted, and she drove her heel into the middle of his abdomen, causing him to curl up again like a pill bug.

"And they have no idea how bad it is," she said. "Today McCormack's CEO sent an email with Wendy's files attached to Jared Thompson at Odyssey Funds. The email said that an open folder with the same files was found on the computer in the home of McCormack's murdered general counsel."

"Why would…" I broke off. Brooke had sent the email.

John said, "Is this the best place to be having this conversation? Let's get the hell out of here."

We both looked at him. He had a point.

"Just a minute." I bent over Marty Nolen and put my hands in his pockets. As I pulled them out, I tossed a key ring, a wallet, and some loose change onto the floor. I bent over the other guy.

"What are you looking for?" Brooke asked.

"Don't know."

Despite the summer heat, the other man was wearing a lightweight jacket over his yellow polo shirt, and beneath it he had a shoulder holster. I pulled out the gun. It was some kind of automatic, but I don't know guns, and that's all I could tell you. I handed it to John.

"What do I want with this?" he said, sounding a bit shrill for a man in my opinion.

I tried to check the pockets of the man's black jeans, but they were so tight on him I could hardly work a hand in. I decided, to heck with it, I'd peruse them at my leisure. He wasn't wearing a belt, and one of his shoes was off already. I unsnapped his jeans and moved to his feet to yank off his remaining shoe.

John said, "What are you doing now? Are you nuts?"

"I'm taking his pants," I said. "What does it look like I'm doing?" I grabbed the end of each pants leg and dragged the man about halfway down the hallway before the pants came off, his shirt rucking up to his armpits and leaving him completely exposed but for his whitey-tighties.

"Let's go," I said, rolling up the jeans so as not to lose anything from the pockets, but when Brooke tried to get past the half-naked man, he grabbed at her ankle and sent her reeling toward me. Already, the man was halfway to his feet, but John pulled back the slide on the automatic pistol, and, as it smacked back in place, the man froze.

"We need to get out of here before we have to kill these people," John said to me.

"This could be the man who killed Wendy," I said, pointing. "He could be the one you're taking the rap for."

"What if he is? What are we going to do about it?"
I thought for a second. "Good point," I said.
Recognizing it, we backed out of there.

Chapter 32

John wanted to go straight to his apartment to get his stuff and maybe clean up a bit, but, halfway there I saw a Mexican restaurant I liked and pulled into the lot. I was starved.

"I've been in jail," John said. "You don't know what that means."

"And you've got blood on your face," Brooke said to him.

"You two are thinking enchiladas," I said, as John's hand went to his face. "Don't."

"What?" John said.

"Think 'pitcher of margaritas.'"

"But you don't drink," John said.

Brooke snorted.

"Let's just say that for the moment I'm operating under a special dispensation."

We went in, sat, and ordered food. The pitcher came almost immediately, and the waitress poured into mugs with salt-encrusted rims. John eyed me as I took a sip, made a face, and took another.

"You girls are out of control," he said, still watching me as he took his first, long swallow. "You know that, don't you? Before this is over, you're going to be in jail, and you'll have lost your license to practice law…"

"Speaking of which, I was in a police lineup today," I said conversationally.

"You…" He reached for his mug.

I told them about it, and their response—both of them, Brooke, too—was stone silence. I gulped from my mug and smacked my lips.

John said, "You're making this up."

Brooke said, "How do you think she came to pick out the secretary?"

"She?" John said. "How do you know the witness was a she?"

"Because Anita Baldridge was the one who saw me in their house last night," I explained.

"You were actually in the Baldridge house?" He looked back and forth between Brooke and me. "I think I spent too much time down the rabbit hole."

To Brooke I said, "Here's my theory. It's not much, but it's all I can come up with. When Anita saw me, I wasn't wearing anything but my red lacy underwear…"

John spewed tequila and lime juice, but I ignored him. "What's the overall impression she got?" I said. "You know, long legs, underwear, her husband's bedroom…"

"Sex pot," Brooke said.

John eyed her.

"And the next time she sees me, I'm like this. Hair pulled back, business attire, face shiny with perspiration. And the girl standing next to me in the lineup…"

"…is a sex pot," Brooke finished.

"Right. Anita picked out the sex pot."

"I think that's it. You've got it."

John said, "You're lesbians, aren't you? You can tell me. I'm cool with it."

For a moment, we both stared at him incredulously. Then Brooke bounced a tortilla chip off his forehead. "Jerk," she said.

John looked at me.

I threw my own chip.

"Are you saying you're not?"

Brooke hit him with another tortilla chip.

From there we went to John's apartment. He needed clothes to go into work the next day, and he needed his car. As hard as it was to believe after all that had been going on, he still had a trial scheduled for the next week.

"Don't forget this week," I said. "The preliminary hearing on your murder charge is Wednesday."

"Fantastic," John said. "You know, because of the weekend I've only missed two days so far, but if this keeps up, Larsen's going to fire my butt."

"I think you've got your priorities mixed up. Virginia still has the death penalty."

"What's that supposed to mean? Are you trying to scare me?"

"Do I need to? Aren't you scared already?"

"Well, sure. I'm terrified. What am I going to do about it, though? I've got a job. I've got clients who are depending on me."

I pulled into the space next to John's car, and we got out. From the ground, his apartment looked fine. On the balcony, neither the loveseat nor the Mexican rug draped over it had been disturbed, and, as we turned the corner, we saw that his front door was closed and intact, as it should be. We mounted the stairs.

I handed John his ring of keys, and he quickly found the right one and opened the door.

Inside the apartment, things were not fine. The first thing to hit us was the smell of stale beer. The sheets and comforter from his bed were in the hallway, and it looked as if a box of Raisin Bran had been emptied on them and then abandoned. I took a step into the apartment, and my foot came down in a puddle of something.

"Oh, gee," Brooke said in an awed voice.

In the galley-style kitchen, the refrigerator had been dumped forward, and it lay tilted against the oven opposite it. John's beer had fallen out, and a couple of the bottles had broken—not nearly enough to account for all the liquid in the front hall, though.

That turned out to be water. Somebody had stuffed one of John's suit coats in the toilet and flushed it multiple times. Most of the contents of his closet seemed to have been relocated to the bathroom floor. Slacks and shirts and ties lay soaked with water, and mixed among them were his razor, his toothbrush, and what seemed to be most of his toiletries.

Not all of his clothes were ruined, fortunately. In the closet there was still a dark gray suit hanging unmolested, a couple of ties, and five shirts still in plastic from the cleaners. A pair of brown dress shoes had also escaped intact.

"Do you have renter's insurance?" I asked John as we looked into the bedroom, where the gutted mattress was on the floor, and the bed frame was broken and sagging.

"No. I don't."

"I'd call the police and the landlord. But not from here, from the hotel. We don't want to spend another evening with the police."

"No," he agreed.

We headed for the door carrying what was left of John's clothes. We'd overlooked the living room on our way in, but there the furniture was overturned and the stuffing from the upholstered pieces was scattered everywhere.

"This is just malicious," John said, pausing in the archway.

"Makes you wonder if we were too gentle with them out at McCormack, doesn't it?"

He only shook his head.

In the parking lot, he unlocked his car door. As Brooke and I were getting into mine, I asked her what she needed from her apartment.

"Nothing," she said. "If they found John's apartment, that means they found mine first. I don't want to know."

John followed us to the hotel. Brooke and I walked through the lobby with him, and we took an elevator up to our floor. Tucking the rolled-up jeans I had stripped from the man at McCormack labs under one arm and shifting John's shoes to my left hand, I slid the card key into the lock and stepped back to let the others enter first.

"This is nice," John said, as he was hanging up the clothes he had salvaged from his apartment. "You've been here how long? It must be setting you back a nice piece of change."

"No," Brooke said. "It hasn't cost us a thing."

He looked at her questioningly.

"I, uh, I have something for you." I put the jeans on the desk and dug John's wallet out of my suitcase. I handed it to him. "I've been holding this for you, remember?"

He looked down at the wallet in his hand, then back up at us. His expression was disbelieving.

"They were looking for us," Brooke said. "We didn't want to use our own names."

"I signed the register as Mrs. John Parker so I could use your card," I said.

"And they didn't question it?"

I shook my head. "Though the card's got your picture on it and everything."

"Well, great," he said.

"I was thinking of it as my legal fee, but I'll reimburse you."

"Mrs. John Parker," he said. "It's like I got stuck with the expense of the wedding, but no honeymoon."

"Get over it," I said. "You had your honeymoon a long time ago."

There was a little awkwardness over the sleeping arrangements. When John was in the bathroom, I asked Brooke if she wanted to sleep with him.

"Are you kidding?"

"I mean share one of the beds. Somebody's got to."

"Somebody's got to share with John?"

Of course no one did; we could share with each other. "You don't find him attractive?"

"It's not that he's unattractive," she said. "It's just

that he's not mine to sleep with."

"Oh, he's every woman's to sleep with. Trust me."

"Great. So potentially, he's a walking cesspool of sexually transmitted diseases."

That was an unpleasant way of putting it, at least to someone who had herself splashed around in the pool. "Now that you put it that way," I said. I got in bed with her.

When John came out of the bathroom, we were lying side-by-side with the covers pulled up to our necks. He stopped short and looked at us. I put my hand out of the covers far enough to wiggle my fingers at him.

"I don't know whether this is sick or kind of exciting," he said.

"Shut up and get in bed," I said.

The next morning I woke to the sound of water running. Brooke was still in bed, lying on her side, her face mashed into the pillow. I raised my head enough to see that John's bed was empty. I lowered my head, and my eyes drifted nearly shut.

When John came out of the bathroom, he had a towel wrapped around his waist. He glanced at us, but both of us were still apparently asleep, I guess. He turned on the light over the sink and started to shave—using, I imagined, one of the safety razors that Brooke or I had left on the side of the tub.

I lay watching him through slitted eyes. He hadn't dried himself very carefully, and there was moisture beaded at the small of his back. Today was Tuesday, which meant that tomorrow was his preliminary hearing, where a district judge would determine whether the Commonwealth of Virginia had probable cause to hold him for trial. Even if the judge found in our favor—and he wouldn't, they never did—it wouldn't put John in the clear. The grand jury could still indict him, and he could be rearrested and tried on the murder charge.

He finished shaving and dried his face with a hand towel. He glanced in our direction, and I lowered my eyelids to cut him off from view. Brooke had rolled onto her back beside me.

Careful not to let my eyebrows move, I opened my eyes again to see John holding the suit pants he had salvaged. Another glance at us, and he dropped the towel.

I heard a small intake of breath beside me.

"Are you two awake?" John said, trying to get his legs into his pants, but stepping on the inside of one pant leg and then the other in his hurry. "For heaven sake." He sounded disgusted. His dangly bits were, well, they were dangling at the top of his thighs.

Beside me, Brooke sat up, and I pushed up on one arm. "Don't you wear underwear?" I asked.

He'd gotten his pants past his knees, turning and giving us both a good look at his buttocks before he got them up all the way. "I couldn't find any underwear last night, if you'll remember. I can't believe this. If I'd been lying there watching you get dressed, you'd be horribly offended."

"Mortified," Brooke said.

I asked, "Are you telling me you wouldn't have looked?"

He just glared at me.

"That's a wool suit," Brooke said. "That's going to be awfully irritating to your skin down there. You'll get a rash."

I said, "You can stop at Wal-Mart on the way into work to pick up a package of underwear."

John was putting on his shirt with quick, jerky movements.

"Oh, don't be mad," I said. I pulled down my T-shirt enough to cover my panties, then threw back the covers and got out of bed. "We're all three crammed into one hotel room together. We can't be overly modest." I walked past him into the bathroom and closed the door.

Just to be on the safe side, I locked it, too.

Chapter 33

We left Brooke in the hotel room. She no longer had a job, but she did have her car there, so it wasn't like we were leaving her stranded.

"You want to ride with me?" I asked John when we got to the parking lot.

"No, I want my own car. That was one of the reasons we went by my place last night, remember?"

"Your call." I followed him out of the parking lot, but lost him when I turned into Burger King to pick up a breakfast sandwich. I had finished it by the time I got on I-64. Once downtown, I wound my way up into the parking garage next to our office building, passing John's car a full level before I found an empty space. He evidently hadn't stopped at Wal-Mart for a package of underwear after all.

I took the parking garage elevator down to the lobby and started across it toward the main elevators. My cell phone rang, and I stopped to get it out of my purse.

It was John.

"There's a cop waiting by the elevators," he said.

"What?"

"There's a cop by the elevators."

I saw him across the lobby. "What do you think he wants?" I asked.

"I didn't ask. He didn't seem interested in me, but I didn't want to push it. Where are you?"

"Looking at the cop." I took a step backward to put him out of sight.

"You're friendly with that policeman who arrested me, aren't you? Jordan?"

"Yesterday he tried to nail me on a murder charge, if you call that friendly."

"Maybe you ought to give him a call to find out what this is about."

"Maybe I ought," I said.

I punched off and looked around. There were a good many people filing through the lobby, but I felt exposed nonetheless. I went into the coffee shop and ordered a latte to sip at one of the high, round tables near the back. When I'd arranged my briefcase and my purse satisfactorily, I called information and let them dial the number for the extra charge. I got put on hold once and transferred twice before I got Jordan.

"This is Robin Starling," I said when he'd identified himself. "What's up?"

"You tell me."

"There's a policeman waiting for me at my office," I said.

"No, there's not."

"Then there's a man here impersonating a policeman. He's standing by the elevators. You can't miss him."

"What makes you think he's looking for you?"

"Isn't he?"

Jordan sighed. "I don't know. Just a minute, I'll see what I can find out."

"Let me give you my number. You can call me back."

After five minutes I began to worry that Jordan might not call back, that he might decide to head me off at my car instead. He'd done it before. I got my stuff together and went back to the parking garage. By the time the phone chirped again, I was out on the street and down to the cold dregs of my latte.

"Tell me you didn't barge into the accounting department at McCormack Labs yesterday and assault the controller of the company," Jordan said.

"Okay."

"Well, he came in last night and swore out a complaint."

"Son of a gun." I saw a parking place along the curb and pulled into it so I could talk without having to mess with traffic.

"Against you and a Brooke Marshall," Jordan said. "Do you know her?"

"Yeah. Do you want to know what really happened?"

"Not particularly. You've been fixated on McCormack since this whole thing started, haven't you?"

"McCormack is bad people. The Brooke Marshall in the warrant—Martin Nolen had her trapped in his office yesterday. When I got there, he attacked me, him and one of his goons." Though it was true, I realized immediately that it was a mistake to say so. I had admitted I was at McCormack just when Nolen said I was, providing one element of the case against me. "Ah, forget it," I said.

"There's a photograph of Nolen attached to the complaint. Somebody sure beat the crap out of him."

"Okay."

"That was you and this Brooke Marshall? What is she, some kind of female sumo wrestler?"

"Actually, she's a petite one-twenty, if that," I said. "For the rest of it, I guess I'd better plead the fifth."

"What's this you say about a goon? The complaint doesn't say anything about another man being there."

"It's possible Marty Nolen was not entirely forthcoming."

"What does this other man look like?"

"Medium height, medium build. Dark hair and fair skin. He may be the one who killed Wendy Walters."

"I meant, did you beat the crap out of him, too? And what do you mean he may have killed Wendy Walters? What do you base that on?"

"A hunch."

"Uh huh. What do you look like?"

"I'm fine."

"You beat the crap out of two men, and you look fine?"

"I'm alleged to have beat the crap out of one man. As you've noticed yourself, the allegation isn't all that credible."

"You want to come in and swear out your own complaint against Nolen?"

I laughed, but it was a bitter laugh. "Heck, no," I said. I tried to think of something else I could say that would help my case, but couldn't come up with anything. I punched *End* and sat back, my head against the headrest, my eyes closed. After a couple of minutes, I opened them again and dialed Brooke at the Marriott.

"Brooke, you need to get out of the hotel." I told her about the arrest warrant that had been issued for the two of us. "I think yesterday, when I was talking to Jordan, I told him where I was staying."

"Well, crap," Brooke said.

"Yeah. Sorry."

"I feel like I'm being hunted."

"You are being hunted."

"What about John?"

"Not named in the warrant."

There was a pause. "He's beautiful, isn't he?"

"John? Yes, he is. That's just what makes him so dangerous to impressionable young women like you and me."

I was waiting for Brooke in the food court at Regency Square Mall when my phone chirped again. John Parker. I answered as I sat at one of the tables.

"It's about time," I said. "For all you knew, I was in lockup."

"So it was you the cop was there for?"

"It was me. Nolen swore out a complaint for criminal assault."

"Where are you now?"

"I'm not sure this is a secure communication," I said. "I'd better not say."

"That's going to make things difficult."

It was. I had, of course, already arranged with Brooke to meet me here, and I'd done it by cell phone. That was going to have to stop.

John said, "Larsen was looking for you. He was in my office for close to half-an-hour."

"What did he want?"

"I don't know. It sounded like that Baldridge guy

was about to throw a chunk of business our way, but he up and died before he could do it."

"Larsen wanted to talk to me about that?"

"Unh huh. He was pretty agitated."

Another reason to stay out of the office. "So what was he doing in your office?"

"I guess he thought I'd know where you were."

"Why would he think that?"

"Because you and I have been sleeping together."

"But no one at the office knows about that," I said.

John's silence provided a complete explanation of the elevator ride I'd had with Steve and his buddies the previous week.

"You blabbermouth," I said.

"So what are you going to do?"

"About the complaint? Spend the day shopping. I don't know."

"You don't have any deadlines coming up, I take it."

"Your preliminary hearing tomorrow at ten."

"Don't you need to prepare for that?"

"Ideally."

"Great."

"It'll be all right. I'll meet you at the courthouse."

"Wait. Where will you be until then?"

"I can't tell you. I thought we'd been over that."

"They're not going to be triangulating your cell phone signal over an assault charge."

"No, probably not, but think just how much it would complicate things if they picked me up. You go back to the Marriott. You can have your own room tonight."

"I'd rather share it with you two."

"Who wouldn't?"

I closed my phone and started to get up, but a hand fell on my shoulder. I yelped as I fell back into my seat.

"Sorry. I didn't want you to get away." It was a good-looking man about my age, dressed in Levi's and a cotton shirt. He pulled out the chair across from me and sat down.

"You don't remember me, do you?" he said.

He did look familiar, but he was right. I didn't.

"Dustin Steed. Steve and I helped you get into your apartment last week."

"Your last name is Steed?" Of course it was.

"I couldn't find you in the phonebook."

"Robin Starling?" I said.

"Ah. Steve said it was Carling, like the beer. Probably because he had a six-pack of it in the cooler out in his truck."

"I guess he had Carling on his mind."

"I guess he did."

"I appreciate your help the other day," I said.

"You're welcome."

We sat looking at each other. I was waiting for him to go. I didn't know what he was waiting for, but I was afraid that, based on our previous encounter, he was waiting for me to disrobe.

He said, "I tried dropping by your apartment one day after work, but you weren't home." That's because he was dropping by Wendy's apartment, of course.

"I moved," I said.

"Where?"

I saw Brooke coming toward me, walking briskly, her red hair swinging. "I gotta go," I said. "Call me.

It'll give you a chance to practice your phonebook skills."

He laughed. "You're on."

He turned and walked away, and I watched him go.

"Who was that?" Brooke asked.

"One of the guys who helped me break into Wendy's apartment the day I discovered her body."

"What's he doing here?"

"Shopping, I guess. I didn't ask him."

"What did he want?"

"My phone number. Evidently, he was impressed by the striptease I did on the balcony in Shockoe Bottom."

"You didn't tell me about doing a striptease."

"Not one of my prouder moments."

We got coffees and Danishes from one of the vendors, and I told her about it.

"It seems like all the guys you know are hunks." She sounded wistful.

"Actually, his friend Steve was the hunky one."

"Hunky and hunkier. It figures."

I balled up my napkin and stood. "We can't stay here," I said. "I doubt they were monitoring my cell phone, but I don't know. I'm far enough behind on technology to make me nervous."

"How about Stony Point Fashion Park?" she suggested. "Switch our operations to the Southside."

I nodded. Another shopping mall seemed like a good place for two women at loose ends. "Okay," I said.

Chapter 34

Since we no longer had John's credit card to pay for it, our accommodations this time was a Budget 8. While Brooke got our stuff out of her car, I went in to register, signing the registration form as Loretta Stevens. Don't ask me where that came from; I haven't a clue. I paid with cash—I'd gotten it from the ATM at the food court—and, as an added precaution, I transposed two of the letters on my license plate.

We each had a bed to ourselves, which made the hotel room seem empty after the night before. We watched TV, catching what might have been the funniest sitcom I've ever seen in my life—at least, I laughed until my sides hurt. Either it was a release from almost unbearable tension, or TV's a lot better than it used to be. You choose.

When the news came on, I noticed the pants I'd taken off the guy at Marty Nolen's office and realized I'd never gone through the pockets.

"Those are that guy's pants," I said.

"Yeah. When I got your call, I packed them up along with everything else."

I got the pants and took them back to the bed. Brooke came over and sat on the end of the bed with her bare legs crossed.

I fished out the wallet. The driver's license had a picture that I wouldn't have recognized, and the name was Armando Gutierrez. I looked at Brooke. "Did he look Hispanic to you?"

She shook her head. "He didn't look like that picture, either."

"Nobody looks like their picture."

"I don't think that's him."

"Well, that's not helpful."

In his right front pocket, Armando, or whatever his name was, had a pocketknife with a six-inch blade that unfolded to the touch of a button. In the pocket with it was a packet of Listerine strips, a little loose change, and a single key. In the other front pocket was a key ring with about a dozen keys on it.

"It could be anybody's pockets," I said.

"Not the knife."

"Okay, the knife's a little much," I agreed. My gaze went from the key ring to the single key. That was odd, too, I thought.

Our wakeup call came at seven. Brooke took it, said thank you, and rolled back onto her back.

"Did you just thank a recorded message?" I asked.

"No, it was a live voice. This is Budget 8, remember."

So it was. After a moment, Brooke said, "No peep show this morning."

"No."

We lay there awhile. Brooked sighed. "He…"

"Don't say it."

"Okay." She sighed again, and I threw a pillow at her.

"Okay, okay." She swung her legs out of bed. "You lie there and think about it. I'm going to take a shower."

She stayed in the bathroom fifteen minutes. My own shower took five. When I came out of the bathroom, I was surprised to find Brooke dressed and putting on her makeup.

"Where are you going?" I asked her.

"To watch you get John off on the murder charge."

"I'm not going to get John off."

"That's not a very positive attitude. Why aren't you going to get him off?"

"Because I can't."

"Because you're not good enough?"

"Well, maybe not. I've never done any criminal work before. But Atticus Finch couldn't get John off today. It's a preliminary hearing. The prosecution doesn't have to prove anything beyond a reasonable doubt. It just has to show probable cause."

"Oh."

"There's no jury, either. The prosecution will put on as few witnesses as it can get away with and summarize as much as possible."

"So the judge is going to find John guilty."

"No. He'll find probable cause to hold him for trial."

She shrugged. "Whatever. I want to see it anyway."

"If the police are there to arrest me, they might pick you up, too."

"They might."

"That would be a bad thing," I pointed out.

"Yes, it would." But she went right ahead working on her face.

I took a breath and sat on the bed, suddenly overwhelmed by the challenges before me. I had no idea what was going to happen in that courtroom or whether I would walk out of it a free woman. Idly, I pulled open the drawer of the nightstand. The Gideon Bible was blue, but otherwise identical to the maroon copy at the Marriott. I picked it up and crossed my legs. I didn't know where to turn in the Bible for words of comfort and inspiration, so I just held it on my lap.

"Dear God," I thought. "Help me to help John Parker." I took a breath. "Whatever it takes." I sat for a while with my mind in idle. *Greater love has no one than this.* I didn't love John Parker, had never loved him with that kind of love. Maybe I never could.

Brooke had turned from the mirror and was watching me. "Are you all right?" she said.

I shrugged, aware suddenly of tears welling in my eyes. I stood abruptly, returned the Bible to the drawer, and pushed it shut. "I feel like I'm playing for all the marbles," I said.

"I guess you are. All John's marbles."

"Maybe mine, too. I can't go home. There's a warrant out for my arrest. People I've never seen before in my life keep popping up out of nowhere to attack me." I sighed. "It's more than that, even. When I'm not too busy to think, I feel almost like a stranger to myself."

"I'm sorry."

I nodded, smiled at her. "Me, too."

Chapter 35

At the courthouse, we parked in the lot and walked around the building to the main entrance. A hot, summer wind whipped our hair and tugged at our skirts. By the time we made it through the revolving door, Brooke looked as though she'd been sitting under an industrial-strength hair dryer. My own hair, fortunately, was in a ponytail, which had protected it from most of the damage. As we joined the line to go through the metal detectors, I used my free hand to smooth the few stray strands of hair back from my face.

In the mirrored elevator, Brooke pushed and patted her own mass of hair into place while the other six people watched her out of the corners of their eyes. We got out on the second floor. John was watching for us from a bench across from the elevators.

When he saw us, he got up and handed me a folder.

"What this?"

"The case file—police reports, medical examiner's report, the rest of it."

"Have you looked through it?"

He nodded.

"Was strangulation the cause of death?"

He rolled his eyes. "Yes, strangulation was the cause of death." He sounded testy. In the ordinary course of events I would have gone through the file meticulously, but you do what you can do.

"Look," John said. "I know the judge is going to bind me over for trial. I just don't want my bail revoked."

"Sure."

"He can do it in a murder case," John said. "Revoke bail."

"I know."

"And you're prepared to handle it?"

"You should have confidence in your legal counsel," I said.

James Jordan got off the elevator at five minutes to ten. A young lawyer from the district attorney's office was with him. I'd met the lawyer before. We'd once sat at the same table at a monthly lunch meeting of the Richmond Bar Association, though I couldn't remember his name.

The two of them came over, and Jordan shook my hand. "Robin," he said.

The lawyer made a chopping motion with his head, the overhead fluorescents glinting in the round lenses of his glasses. "Ian Maxwell," he said.

"Are you out on bail, or have they not caught up with you yet?" Jordan asked me.

I felt my mouth stretch, but I didn't say anything. Ian didn't react either, which told me he knew all about my arrest warrant already. We went into the clerk's office together, and the clerk nodded us through to a small courtroom.

The judge wasn't at the bench, and the courtroom was empty. John and I sat at the counsel table furthest from the door, and Brooke sat behind us in one of only a dozen chairs provided for spectators. Jordan and Ian Maxwell took the other table, Maxwell taking a folder out of his briefcase and squaring it neatly on the tabletop.

A man with a mustache and thinning red hair opened a door, looked at us, and disappeared again. A few moments later the judge came in. His name was Cochran. I didn't know him, but he appeared to be only a couple of years older than I was. He had short, dark hair and a goatee that caused his chin to disappear against his black robe when he bent his head. "State versus John Parker," he read.

The red-haired man came in and took his place at the Stenotype.

"Is the state ready?" the judge asked.

Ian Maxwell stood up. "Ready."

"I don't believe I know you, Counselor."

"Ian Maxwell, Your Honor."

"Pleased to meet you. Is the defense ready?"

I stood. "Ready. Robin Starling, Your Honor."

"Is the defendant present?"

John stood. "Present."

"Your name is John Wesley Parker?" the judge asked him.

"Yes, Your Honor."

"You're represented by Robin Starling? Do you understand that this is a preliminary hearing?"

He was, and he did.

"Has your lawyer explained to you the nature and purpose of a preliminary hearing?"

She hadn't, but it hadn't been necessary. "Yes, she has," John said.

"You understand that you are accused of murdering Wendy Walters sometime late August twelfth or early in the morning of August thirteenth."

John nodded. "Yes."

"It is your right to make a statement relative to this accusation. Do you wish to make such a statement, understanding that you cannot be compelled to do so and that any statement you make may be used in evidence against you?"

"No, Your Honor."

A uniformed police officer had come in and joined Jordan and Maxwell at their table. The judge said to Maxwell, "Call your witnesses."

Maxwell called the uniformed cop, a young man named Jason Booth. On the afternoon of August 13, Booth had gotten a call from the dispatcher at 12:25 and, as a result of that call, had gone with his partner to 1901-B Main Street, the apartment above Joe's Diner.

"And what did you find there?" Maxwell asked.

"The door was locked. We watched a woman come down the stairs, and she let us in."

"Did she use a key?"

"Yes. The lock was a double-keyed deadbolt. She used a key on a key ring."

"Who was the woman? Did you subsequently identify her?"

"Yes, sir. It was Robin Starling. That woman there." He pointed at me.

The judge's eyebrows rose. I ignored the frown he gave me.

"What happened then?" Maxwell asked.

"We followed her up the stairs."

"What did you find?"

"A dead woman, about age thirty. She was lying on the couch in the living room with a wire around her neck."

"What was she wearing?"

"Just her underwear."

"A bra and panties?"

"Yes."

Maxwell looked at me. "Your witness."

I didn't stand. "Describe the wire you found around her neck."

"It was telephone wire. Light gray."

"No further questions."

John's eyes cut toward me. I ignored him, too.

Jordan was next. The judge swore him in, and he sat down.

"Were you at 1901-B Main Street on August 13th?"

"I was."

"How did you come to be there?"

"I went in response to a call from the dispatcher. My partner, Ray Hernandez, was with me."

"What did you find?"

His description matched Booth's, and he, too, identified me as the woman on the scene.

"Just a minute," the judge said, interrupting. "Do you intend to call Ms. Starling as a witness?"

"Not at this time, Your Honor," Maxwell said.

The judge pursed his mouth. Since hearsay was inadmissible, even in a preliminary hearing, Jordan couldn't testify to anything I'd told him. To the judge that might have looked like a problem, but, unfortunately, the prosecution didn't need my testimony to implicate John.

Judge Cochran said to me, "Ms. Starling, it seems clear to me that you will be called as a witness when this gets to trial."

I stood. "Yes, Your Honor."

He looked at John. "Between now and then, you're going to have to find other counsel. You realize that, don't you?"

John stood next to me. In my experience, judges can't hear you unless you stand up. "I'm aware that it's likely, Your Honor."

"I understand you're a lawyer yourself. Is that correct?"

"I've practiced law in Richmond for six years."

The judge looked as if he had more to say, but in the end he only nodded. "Proceed, Counselor," he said to Maxwell.

"How long have you been with the police force, Mr. Jordan?"

"Twenty-two years."

"You're currently in the homicide division?"

He was. He had investigated more than one hundred fifty homicides. He was familiar with crime scene investigations and had experience in fingerprinting and ballistics. The point of all this testimony was to qualify him as an expert, which meant that at some point Maxwell was going to ask him for an opinion.

"Did you ever identify the decedent?" Maxwell asked.

"We did. She is Wendy Walters, a thirty-one-year-old accountant with McCormack Labs."

"How did you come to make that identification?"

"Counsel for the defense identified her." It earned me another frown from the judge. "Also, there was a purse in the apartment with a wallet containing both a driver's license and a credit card with a photograph on it. The pictures of Wendy Walters were that of the dead woman."

"Whose apartment was this where you found her?"

"It was leased to Wendy Walters."

"So she was found in her own home."

I stood. "Is Mr. Maxwell relying on Officer Jordan's status as an expert to draw this conclusion, or are we just stating the obvious?" I said.

Maxwell withdrew the question, and I sat down. John leaned toward me. "Was there a point to that?"

"Just letting them know I'm alive."

His eyes rolled briefly upward as he sat back.

"Was the apartment dusted for fingerprints?" Maxwell asked.

"It was."

"Whose did you find there?"

I stood up again. "I'm concerned about Mr. Maxwell's use of the passive voice in the previous question. He's elicited the response that the apartment was dusted. Officer Jordan didn't say he dusted it."

"I didn't," Jordan said. "Not personally."

"Impersonally?" I said. "I think it's important that we establish the source of Mr. Jordan's knowledge."

The judge looked at Maxwell, who nodded. If you're not familiar with courtroom procedure, this kind of crap goes on all the time. You get used to it. The point is to make sure that any evidence presented has a factual basis.

"Mr. Jordan?" Maxwell asked him.

"A team of technicians working under my direction dusted the apartment for fingerprints. Together we compared the prints recovered to those of the defendant John Parker."

I stood up again. "What does he mean by 'under his direction'? While the crime techs were dusting for prints, isn't it a fact that Detective Jordan was sitting at the kitchen table talking to me?"

The judge looked at Jordan.

"That's true," Jordan said. "What I meant was that they reported to me."

"And at some point," I said, "they presented him with prints that they said came from the apartment. He doesn't know where they came from of his own knowledge. What he's giving us implicitly are the hearsay statements made to him by these crime techs."

The judge said, "Mr. Maxwell?"

Maxwell sighed. "If you'll give me a fifteen minute recess, Your Honor, I can produce one of the technicians."

The judge nodded and, without speaking, stood and left the bench. Maxwell got on his cell phone, and we listened to him arrange for the lab tech to get over to the courtroom pronto.

"I'm probably going to need the M.E., too," he said, flipping through his papers. "Pavlicek signed the autopsy report. Can you get him here in thirty?"

Sitting back with a sense of some satisfaction, I looked at John and raised my eyebrows.

"You've got something in mind?" he said.

"I'm making them prove their case."

He took a deep breath and let it out slowly.

"What?" I said.

"Much ado about nothing."

Thank you, William Shakespeare. "Look," I said. "It's my job to get a look at as many of their witnesses as possible. If I'm not going to do that, we might as well waive the preliminary hearing altogether."

John nodded, his lips compressed, and looked away.

Chapter 36

The lab tech was a huge brute of a man in his mid-twenties. Now that I saw him, I remembered him from the crime scene. His face was square and angular, handsome on a gargantuan scale.

"Your name?" Maxwell asked him, when he'd been sworn in and had taken his seat.

"Danny Golden." His voice was a deep bass that matched his frame.

"Did you have occasion to visit 1901-B Main Street on the day of August 13th?"

He had, of course. Maxwell led him through the preliminaries. Golden had himself dusted for prints and recorded the locations. He had himself made the print comparisons, with James Jordan watching.

"Did you take any prints from the Wendy Walters apartment that you subsequently identified as belonging to the defendant, John Parker?"

"Yes," Golden rumbled. "We found prints of all five fingers of Parker's right hand and prints of his left thumb and middle finger."

Maxwell looked at me. "Your witness."

I stood. "When were the prints in the apartment made?"

Golden shrugged.

"Could you say the prints were made the previous evening?" I asked.

"There's no way to tell when they were made," he said.

"For all you know, each of the prints you found could have been there a week. Or longer."

His big head nodded. "For all I know," he said.

"Did you find anybody else's prints?"

"The decedent's, Wendy Walters's. And yours."

"My prints were in the apartment?"

"The second, third, and fourth fingers of your right hand."

"No further questions."

The judge said, "Ms. Starling." He hesitated, then shook his head.

I sat down just as a small man in a hounds-tooth sports jacket entered the courtroom. Maxwell introduced him as Dr. Harold Pavlicek. The judge swore him in, and Maxwell had the doctor identify himself for the record. Pavlicek was a board-certified pathologist who had gone to the Medical College of Virginia right there in Richmond before going to Orlando, Florida, for a five-year residency. He estimated that he had performed something over a thousand autopsies.

"Did you have cause to examine one Wendy Walters on the day of August 13th?"

"I did. As the result of a phone call, I arrived at an apartment in the 1900 block of Main Street shortly before two o'clock p.m."

"And what did you find there?"

"A young Caucasian female, about thirty-years of age, deceased."

"Where was the body exactly?"

"Lying in the supine position on a sofa in the front room of the apartment."

"This was Wendy Walters?"

"That is my understanding. Wendy Walters was the name on her driver's license."

"What was the condition of the body?"

"She had been dead for some time, I would say some fourteen hours, give or take an hour-and-a-half. There was a ligature about her neck…"

"A what?"

"A cord of some kind. Her face was congested. There were abrasions on the neck and contusions of the underlying tissues—a ligature mark."

"What was the cause of death?"

"Occlusion of the vessels supplying blood and oxygen to the brain."

Maxwell hesitated.

"Constriction of the neck by ligature," the doctor added helpfully.

"Was she raped?"

"In cases of strangulation—most cases involve women—rape always has to be ruled out. But in this case, I would say she was not raped."

"She had not had intercourse recently?"

The doctor's smile was thin. "I didn't say that. There were no abrasions or contusions of the thighs and external genitalia. Their absence would be unusual if rape were the case."

"But she had engaged in intercourse recently."

"She wasn't raped."

"She'd had consensual intercourse," Maxwell said, a hint of exasperation creeping into his tone.

"In my opinion."

"How do you know?"

"There were traces of semen still in the vagina."

I felt my lip curl. I glanced at John, whose gaze was fixed on the doctor, his face reddening. I was glad to see he had some shame.

"Did you conduct any tests on the semen you found?" Maxwell asked.

"Yes."

"Did you conduct a DNA test?"

"Yes. The results of that test became available just this morning. The DNA of the semen was a match to the blood sample provided to me."

Maxwell looked at the judge. "Your Honor, I'll wait to establish the chain of custody, if that's all right."

He got a nod, which meant he wouldn't have to stop and deal with the source of the blood sample right then.

"Dr. Pavlicek. You said that death had occurred fourteen hours or so prior to your examination. That was at roughly two o'clock in the afternoon?"

"That's right."

"So the time of death…"

"Would have been sometime between ten-thirty p.m. the evening of the twelfth and one-thirty a.m. the morning of the thirteenth."

"How did you establish the time of death?"

"Ah. Yes." Dr. Pavlicek pulled some stapled pages from the inside pocket of his jacket and unfolded them.

"Is that the autopsy report?" I said.

The doctor looked up, blinking. John slid our copy across the table to me.

"Is that a copy of the autopsy report?" Maxwell asked the witness.

"Yes. Yes, this is the report of my postmortem examination." Dr. Pavlicek cleared his throat and turned a couple of pages, his eyes scanning. "Ah. Rigor mortis was fully developed; postmortem lividity was fully established and fixed." He glanced up. "Both conditions together suggest that death had occurred at least ten to twelve hours previously. At 2:25 the temperature of the body was 77.8 degrees. Given the temperature of the room where the body was found—it was 72 degrees, air-conditioned—I would expect it to have lost 1.5 degrees Fahrenheit for each hour after death. Since normal rectal temperature is between ninety-nine and one hundred degrees…"

There was more, including something about finding Wendy's last meal in her large intestine, which was more than I wanted to know. When I thought of her, images of her lying dead on the sofa in her apartment were intermingled with images of her in my office wearing business attire and images of a younger Wendy in a basketball uniform. She'd been a great point guard, with hands so fast she could steal the ball and be halfway down the court before any of us realized what was happening.

"Do you have any questions, Ms. Starling?" the judge asked.

I started, then glanced around, unsure how long I had been zoned out.

"No questions," I said.

Chapter 37

Maxwell called James Jordan back to the stand. When it was my turn to have a crack at him, I stood, aware of John looking up at me. "Detective Jordan, Mr. Golden testified that it is impossible to tell from the physical evidence when the fingerprints found in Wendy's apartment were made. Do you agree with that testimony?"

"I would, but your client has admitted to being in the apartment that night."

"He said that he took her home."

"And went into the apartment."

"So the presence of his fingerprints is consistent with his statement."

"Yes."

"And his statement also provides us with an entirely innocent explanation of his presence in the apartment."

Jordan didn't answer, but then, I hadn't really asked a question. I felt an interior nudge, the beginnings of an idea.

"What kind of lock is on the outside door of the decedent's apartment?" I asked.

"A double-keyed deadbolt."

"Is that a lock that requires a key to lock or unlock it, even from the inside?"

"That's right."

"So if the door was locked after Mr. Parker left the apartment, that would have to have been done with a key."

"That's right," Jordan said.

"Wendy Walters could have let him out herself and locked up behind him—isn't that right?"

"If she were alive, of course, she could have done that. She wouldn't have needed to, though. Mr. Parker had a key. We found it on the dresser inside his apartment."

"If she had given him a key…"

"We don't think she gave him the key."

"That sounds like an opinion. Does your expertise extend to determining when and how the key to a young woman's apartment might come into a man's possession?"

"There was a small nail in the molding of the door at the top of the stairs that led down to the outside door. There was no key on it. Our theory is that the killer took the key on his way out of the apartment."

"So now your expertise extends to the purpose and habitual uses of small nails in door moldings," I said.

The judge interrupted me. "You've made your point, Ms. Starling. We'll strike the opinion testimony from the record."

"Thank you, Your Honor." To Jordan I said, "I gather from your testimony that you searched Mr. Parker's apartment."

"We did."

"Did you find evidence that anyone was living with Mr. Parker? A second toothbrush, some clothes, anything like that?"

Jordan shifted in his chair, glancing at Maxwell. "We did."

"What did you find, specifically?"

"A toothbrush. Some clothes."

"How did you know the clothes didn't belong to Mr. Parker himself?"

"The clothes included a pair of women's jeans, a few blouses, a bra, and a couple of pairs of panties."

"I take it the clothes wouldn't have fit Mr. Parker? He's not a cross-dresser?" Beside me, John gave a small grunt of annoyance.

"Frankly, the possibility didn't occur to us. We also found some cosmetics and a box of tampons under the sink."

"So a woman was living with Mr. Parker, or at least spending the night occasionally. Was it Wendy Walters?"

"We don't think so."

"Why not? Was there a name sewed into the underwear?" You may have noticed that I have a weakness for sarcasm. In court, it's gotten me into trouble more than once.

"Mr. Parker said that she visited him for the first time on August twelfth," Jordan said.

"He also told you he didn't kill Wendy Walters," I said. "And yet, here we are."

He turned his hands palms up. "Here we are," he said.

"Did you find Ms. Walters's fingerprints in John Parker's apartment?"

"Yes. On an interior doorknob and on the coffee

table, I believe."

"Ah."

"Not the volume of prints we would have expected if she were living there."

"But evidently some woman was a regular guest. She must have left prints."

"There were lots of prints we didn't identify."

"John Parker's prints?"

"I would assume so. We didn't make the comparisons."

"My prints?"

He was silent for several seconds. "I don't know."

"So far as you know then, all the prints in that apartment that didn't belong to Wendy Walters were John Parker's."

"So far as we know."

"But the clothes and cosmetics and so on suggest that John Parker had a girlfriend."

"Yes."

"And his statement indicates that it wasn't Wendy Walters."

"That's right."

"So," I said, "in injecting his DNA sample into Ms. Walters, Mr. Parker was cheating on a girlfriend." I turned to look at the culprit. John's flushed face seemed to have turned to wood, but I didn't let it worry me. I was on a roll.

"Detective Jordan," I said. "Let me propound to you a hypothetical. Let us say that John Parker was cheating on his girlfriend, and his girlfriend was aware of it. She followed John and Wendy to Ms. Walters's apartment on the night of her death and sat outside, watching their shadows on the window blinds. As she sat there, she found herself getting more and more angry. When she saw her two-timing boyfriend leave..." I smiled at the two-timing boyfriend in question. "...she knocked on the door and convinced Wendy Walters to let her in. Once inside, Mr. Parker's girlfriend strangled Ms. Walters and arranged her on the couch. Then she left, taking the key from the small nail at the top of the stairs and locking up after herself."

I had everyone's attention. They were all staring at me as if I were deranged.

I asked, "Is there anything in the physical evidence that would rule out such a possibility?"

"Your client was the one who had the key," Jordan said.

"Of course he had a key!" I shouted. "He was sleeping with the little slut!"

Everyone in the courtroom seemed to have gone into shock. The judge opened his mouth, but closed it again without speaking.

In a lower voice, I said, "You don't have any basis at all for assuming the key you found in his apartment was the one that came from that nail at the top of the stairs. Do you?"

He didn't answer.

"Do you, Mr. Jordan?"

"We haven't found another key."

"Suppose you found another woman's fingerprints inside Wendy Walters's apartment. Suppose that woman was the girlfriend whose clothing you found in John Parker's apartment. Suppose it turned out that this girlfriend also has a key to Wendy Walters's apartment."

Jordan smiled, a little weakly. "That's a lot of supposes," he said.

"There's nothing in the physical evidence to contradict it. Is there?"

"We don't know of another woman's prints inside the Walters apartment."

"Weren't you in the courtroom when Mr. Golden testified?"

He didn't answer.

"Mr. Golden testified that he found prints of the second, third, and fourth fingers of my right hand. Didn't he?"

"Yes."

"I was in the apartment when you got there. You took my prints to rule them out, didn't you?"

"Yes."

"Yet according to your testimony, you didn't compare my prints to the prints you found in John Parker's apartment. Did you?"

"No."

"Suppose they matched," I said. "Suppose it turned out that there was a key, a key to Wendy Walter's apartment, in my possession." The skirt of my dress had pockets, and in one of them I had the key I had taken from the pants of Armando Gutierrez. I didn't know what it was a key to, but I took it out and laid it on the rail by the witness stand. James Jordan looked at it. The judge looked at it. Then both of them raised their gazes to look at me.

"No further questions," I said, and I sat down.

The silence in the courtroom went on for longer than I would have thought possible. Finally, the judge said, "Do you mean to tell me..." He held up a hand, forestalling an answer. "Never mind. I don't want to hear it." He continued to stare at me for a long moment. Finally, he turned his gaze to Maxwell. "Do you have any more questions for this witness?"

Maxwell's eyes cut to me. "No, Your Honor."

"Anything else? Any more witnesses?"

Maxwell shook his head. "The prosecution rests."

"Are you going to put on a defense?" the judge asked me. "I don't recommend it."

"I guess I'm done, then."

"I'm going to take a fifteen minute recess." He picked up his gavel and let it fall. Then he was up and out of the courtroom.

"What was all that about?" John said, so softly that his voice was barely audible even in the silenced courtroom.

Brooke touched my shoulder. "What are you doing?"

"Representing a client." *Greater love has no one than this*, I thought.

John said, "I'm not sure this was the place for that bombshell. You won't be able to pull the same stunt when we get to trial."

"One thing at a time," I said. "And, anyway, I'm going to be a witness when this comes to trial. I won't be your attorney." I looked up at Jordan, who was standing in front of my table.

"Where did you get the key?" Jordan asked me.

"Does it matter?"

"We know the killer had one," Jordan said, "because he was able to lock up after himself. Or herself."

"It's beginning to look as if there were keys floating all over the place, doesn't it?"

Jordan nodded. "There's still an arrest warrant outstanding for you," he said.

"Are you arresting me?"

"Just don't plan on going anywhere when this trial's over."

He went to the other table.

"Now you've done it," John said. "Both of us are going to jail."

"I have a key, and arguably I had motive. You had a key, and arguably you had motive. I don't think they can make this stick against either one of us, unless they can tie that telephone cord to someone."

"So to speak," John said.

Brooke said, "It sounds like they're about to arrest you for assaulting Martin Nolen. Me, too, I guess."

"Yes. You probably ought to get out of here."

She didn't though. The three of us sat waiting for the judge. At the prosecution's table Maxwell and Jordan were whispering together, but about what I couldn't speculate. I was about to be arrested, fingerprinted, and photographed, and, though I had done it to myself, I didn't like it.

I stood abruptly. "I'm going to the restroom."

John looked alarmed. "What? Now?"

"When a girl's got to go," I said.

"I'll go with you." Brooke picked up her purse. I hesitated a moment, then nodded.

As we walked past the prosecutor's table, Jordan made eye contact and raised his eyebrows.

"Restroom," I said, and we went out.

The door to the stairs was right outside the courtroom. As we went by it, I glanced back over my shoulder. Jordan was standing in the courtroom doorway, watching us.

The women's room was at the other end of the floor, past the elevators. We went in, and Brooke took the first stall. I went over to the windows and looked north to the parking lot where Brooke and I had left my car.

We were just on the second floor, but the tinted windows weren't made to open. There was no escape that way. It was ridiculous that I was even thinking of such a thing, of course. A week ago, escape wouldn't even have occurred to me as a possible course of action. For days, though, I had been on the run, hopping from place to place in an effort to stay ahead of police and bad guys both. And for days the strategy had worked pretty well.

A toilet flushed, and Brooke came out of the stall. "What are you doing?"

"Thinking."

"You don't need to go?"

"Not really. I'm just antsy. I'm not looking forward to spending the rest of the day in jail."

"Me either."

"What do you suggest?" I asked.

She shrugged. "I dunno."

"I don't know either."

When we came out of the restroom, we could see Jordan at the other end of the hall, now standing in front of the clerk's office. He nodded at us.

"He's thinking we might cut and run," I said softly to Brooke.

There was another stairway at this end of the floor, across from the women's room. I was surprised Jordan hadn't positioned himself in front of it. Actually, I was just as surprised at myself for walking past it. I didn't know whether Jordan would arrest me immediately on Nolen's warrant or whether he would wait to swear out a new warrant for Wendy Walters's murder. It was possible, of course, that I wouldn't be arrested at all, but I wasn't counting on it.

The elevator opened as we were passing it, and a man stepped off. On impulse, I grabbed Brooke's arm and stepped into the open cab, pulling her with me. I heard my name shouted and caught a glimpse of Jordan as the doors closed. The elevator started moving.

Brooke looked at me wide-eyed. I shrugged and made a face. "It would be nice to say I know what I'm doing," I said.

"But you don't."

"I'm trying to stay one step ahead of everybody else. I can't do that in jail."

The elevator door opened. I hustled Brooke out. "Jordan's going to be coming down the stairs," I said. I let go of her, and we walked swiftly across the lobby, our heels clacking on the tile.

"When are we going to hear something from that guy at Odyssey Funds?" I asked conversationally. We pushed through the revolving door into the heat.

"Jared Thompson?" Brooke said. "I don't know that we're going to hear anything."

"I don't mean directly—but he got the information on Monday. Eventually, he'll be making a statement or selling shares or something."

"Selling shares based on nonpublic information would be insider trading," Brooke said. "It's illegal." A couple of steps brought us to the sidewalk, and we turned to skirt the building. "And he might just delete the message without opening the attachments, you know. A lot of people do that."

"Now that's encouraging." We were moving down the sidewalk as quickly as two women in heels and tailored dresses can move—which wasn't very. I heard a shout from behind us.

"Come on," I said to Brooke. I pulled up my dress to the top of my legs and started to run.

Brooke hesitated, but caught up with me almost immediately. Because of our heels, we had to run on our toes, but our speed improved considerably. We crossed the street to the parking lot just as the light changed and released a flow of traffic. As I beeped my car and grabbed the door handle, I saw Jordan start into the traffic and jerk back onto the curb as a horn blared.

I swung down into the car and keyed the ignition.

"What now?" Brooke asked me as she swung into her own seat.

"Heck if I know."

"I mean, where are we going?"

"Heck if I know that either." I glanced at her as I backed out of the space. Jordan was crossing the street toward us. "You worried?"

"Heck, yes."

I wiggled my fingers at Jordan as we drove past him, and he shook his head in evident exasperation. For some reason, that gave both Brooke and me the giggles.

Chapter 38

We were on I-64 when my cell phone rang. The best plan I had come up with was to find a motel up in Ashland or Fredericksburg or somewhere that would rent a room to us by the week. I didn't know how long it would keep us out of jail. It might give us the time for one critical play, if I could figure out what that play should be.

"We're going to be living out of a suitcase for longer than we thought," I said. "We're going to need more stuff."

"Drop by your place, then mine?" Brooke said.

"And go by the ATM to get a wad of cash. Four hundred for me, four hundred for you, and that's it for the duration. They'll be able to track where we are when we make withdrawals."

My cell phone kept chirping, and Brooke said, "Aren't you going to pick it up?"

"Yeah, I guess." I didn't recognize the number, but it had to be either John or Jordan.

"Robin Starling," I said.

It was John, calling from the courthouse phone.

"Where are you?" he asked.

I sighed. "Where I always am. On the run. What happened?"

"I've been released from bail."

"What?"

"The judge said it was a close question, but that he'd heard two people implicated in the courtroom and frankly thought Maxwell had a stronger case against the defendant's attorney. It probably helped that you resorted to flight.'"

"Ah, good. Glad I've accomplished something."

"It's not like Judge Cochran's is the last word. The grand jury can always indict me, and the prosecution can continue almost without a blip."

"Too true."

"From listening to Maxwell and Jordan, I think they may be getting a warrant out for you."

I was silent for a few seconds. "Well," I said. "I expected it."

"Why did you do it, Robin? It doesn't make any sense for you to implicate yourself."

"I didn't intend to, starting out. It just kind of came to me as I went along, and I went with the flow." I thought of my prayer that morning. *Whatever it takes.* There was no real reason to assume a connection, but from now on I was going to be much more careful what I prayed for.

"You were amazing," John said. "I don't think one lawyer in fifty could have pulled that off."

I felt a rush of gratitude, but I said, "Why quibble? Why not one in a million?" I heard an unexpected tremor in my voice and punched off abruptly, afraid I was about to start blubbering.

Brooke said, "Are you all right?"

I nodded, my eyes streaming tears.

"Do you want me to drive?"

I shook my head and wiped at my eyes with the heel of my hand. I think I'd have felt better if I had any idea of what to do next.

Chapter 39

From the alley behind my house, I turned into the driveway. The garage door rumbled up, I drove in, and the garage door rumbled down behind us. "Keep a low profile," I said. "In and out. Nobody will know we were here."

"Sounds good."

Somehow most of my lamebrain ideas do. We were in the bedroom, a half-filled suitcase open on the bed, when we heard a sound from the living room.

"Uh oh," Brooke said.

"No." I reached across the bed to pick up the phone, but there was no dial tone, and my cell phone was in the car. "No, no, no."

Marty Nolen appeared in the doorway, holding some kind of revolver. It was the gun that caught and held our attention. "I think you ladies might want to come into the living room," he said. He raised the gun and thumbed back the hammer. I cringed, flinging up a hand and turning my head away, but he didn't fire.

"No fuss now, or I'll shoot you and drag you."

We went, and he backed out ahead of us. Armando Gutierrez was in the living room, as was a man I'd never seen before who was standing with his hands in his pockets. Armando was on the couch, sitting forward with his forearms on his thighs, a pistol dangling carelessly from his hand.

"There's the girl took my pants," Armando said, looking up.

The man with his hands in his pockets said, "Hell with your pants. She killed Tony."

I thought of the man I'd stabbed with the corkscrew, and dread settled like a brick deep in my guts. "What do you want?" I asked, and my voice quavered.

"Oh, I think you know what we want," Marty said from behind us. "Keep moving."

We took another couple of steps forward.

Armando got up. "How we gonna do this?"

I felt the barrel of Marty's revolver just under my ear, and my mouth went dry.

"I want this one to sit on the end of the coffee table," Marty said.

He pushed. I recovered my balance, turned, and sat. It was a sturdy coffee table, solid wood with stout, round legs.

"Lie back on the table," Marty said. I looked around at him, and he smiled. The barrel of the gun was pointed at the middle of my forehead.

I lay back on the altar, wishing I wasn't wearing a dress.

"Hands touching the floor."

I let them touch the floor on either side of me.

"You, sit," the nameless man said to Brooke, and he pushed her into my club chair.

"Tie her up," Marty said to Armando, jerking his head at me.

Armando knelt beside me. My options, I felt, were fast disappearing, but with a gun trained on me from half-a-dozen feet away, it was hard to see what options I had in the first place. Moving with practiced speed, Armando looped something around one of my wrists and then the other, and drew the cord tight enough beneath the table that I felt the strain in my shoulders. The pain was so great that I stopped worrying about people looking up my dress.

"Don't hurt her," Brooke said, sounding as if she were close to tears.

Armando moved to the end of the coffee table to lash a cord around my feet. He threw the end of the cord under the table and, going around to my head, picked it up and pulled my feet toward him. He looped the other end of the cord around my neck and tied it.

I started to choke almost immediately and could relieve the pressure on my throat only by curling my feet under me as far as the frame of the table would allow.

"You're killing her." It was Brooke's voice, followed by a slap that must have turned her head on her shoulders.

"Now we're going to talk," Marty said. "You and me."

He was outside my field of vision, and I wasn't sure whether he was talking to Brooke or to me. I was concentrating on breathing, in any case. My world had gotten suddenly very small.

Marty said, "I want to know where Wendy's disc is. I want to know what copies you've made and where to find them—and I want to know who's seen them."

"Okay," Brooke said. "Okay, I'll tell you. Anything. Just don't hurt her."

My left hamstring cramped, and my leg started to straighten automatically. I gagged, curled my cramping leg under me again, and gritted my teeth against the pain that spread upward from the back of my thigh into my left buttock. I breathed one gasping breath at a time, and Brooke's voice flowed over me. Her purse in the car, she said. There was a disc there. A copy of the files was on her computer; that was in the car, too. She'd emailed Jared Thompson at Odyssey Funds a copy. She didn't know Thompson, and she hadn't spoken to him. She'd just sent him an email and had no idea whether he had gotten it or had deleted it without opening the attachment.

I closed my eyes, not able to wonder whether Brooke was putting Jared Thompson in jeopardy, but concentrating only on keeping my knees bent and my air passage open.

The front door banged open. There was a cry of exclamation and a voice like the voice of God, except that it was cracked with age—a timbre that might not disqualify it, since God himself is reputed to be no spring chicken. There were gunshots. I opened my eyes and saw old Dr. McDermott standing backlit in the front doorway just as someone fell across me, his weight landing on my chest and stomach. The air gusted out of my lungs with a grunt, my arms and legs surged against the cords that held them, and the garrote tightened about my throat and closed off my airway.

There were two more gunshots, and a woman's cry.

My mouth gaped uselessly. With the man on top of me, I couldn't recover. Black patches sprang into the air above me, and it occurred to me that I was dying. I felt hands on my ankles, pushing at them.

And, just before I passed out, I heard sirens.

Chapter 40

Dr. McDermott and I went to St. Mary's Hospital in the same ambulance. I was in the emergency room when I regained consciousness, but later they told me that in the ambulance Dr. McDermott had tried to doctor me, even while strapped to a gurney in the supine position. He demanded information the paramedics wouldn't give him and gave orders they didn't obey. Their placatory assurances irritated him beyond endurance, and he kept raising his head to look at me, though my oxygen mask obscured my face.

"I'm a physician, blast it," he said, "the only one in this vehicle." He paid no attention at all to the bullet in his right leg and showed no interest in its treatment.

When I opened my eyes, Brooke was sitting in a plastic chair inside the curtained cubicle with me. She popped out of the chair immediately and laid a hand on my arm. "How do you feel?"

I tried to speak, but my voice sounded like a frog's would if a frog could talk.

"It's all right," Brooke said.

"Tell. Me," I croaked.

"That old man from across the street saved us."

"Dr. Mmm…" I gave up. McDermott was too much for my tortured throat.

"The door slammed open, and there he was," Brooke said. "He took in everything at a glance, and he started shooting."

I smiled weakly, remembering the glimpse I'd had of him with the light around him. An avenging angel.

"If he'd hesitated, they'd have got him—probably would have killed all of us—but he got all three of them. Actually, I think one of them's still alive—Armando, the guy whose pants you took. At least, they were loading him into another ambulance when I left to follow yours. All three of our attackers were down before Marty Nolen got the shot off that hit your doctor friend in the leg. He staggered, shot Marty in the head, then fell down." She shivered suddenly. "It was pretty awful, really. Marty's head…"

"Doctor…"

"He's in surgery now," Brooke said.

I closed my eyes.

The skin on my neck was raw and bleeding a little, and my throat was badly bruised. A uniformed policeman came and went, but my contribution to his report consisted of little more than the occasional nod in support of Brooke's statements. Though I was sitting up and sipping ice water, I was unable to speak above a whisper.

When Dr. McDermott was out of surgery and in the recovery room, the uniformed policeman came back by to talk to us. The surgeon had informed the police that he'd gotten the bullet out with no damage to "that big artery down there or the nerve or anything," according to the cop. Evidently, the bullet had lodged in the soft tissue of McDermott's upper thigh without doing any major damage. I tried for further details, but the cop had given us what he knew.

"I hear one of the guys he shot's likely to make it, too, though he's still in surgery."

"Where..." I gave it up.

"Two in the chest is what I heard. You know, you should rest your voice."

"Thanks for the tip," I whispered hoarsely.

The cop laughed and squeezed my knee.

"He was nice," Brooke said when he had gone. "No wedding ring."

I raised an eyebrow, but Brooke ignored it.

"I followed the ambulance in your car, so it's here," she said. "Your purse, too." It, as well as her own purse, was sitting on the chair beside her. "Maybe we could go by an ice cream place when we get out of here. Ice cream will feel good on that throat of yours."

I didn't think so, but I nodded.

By the time the hospital released me, Dr. McDermott had been checked into the hospital and was in his room. And my throat had closed up to the point that I couldn't talk at all.

I made writing gestures with my hand, and Brooke got some paper and a pen from one of the clerks at the registration desk. I sat at a small table in the waiting room and wrote out a few messages in block letters. Then we went to find Dr. McDermott.

He was half-sitting in his bed, propped on his pillows. His face was gray, and the wattled skin on his neck hung slackly, but he rallied when he saw us in the doorway.

Standing by the bed, I held up a sheet of paper. "THANKS. YOU WERE GREAT." I could feel tears on my face.

"She can't talk," Brooke said. "Her throat's all bruised up."

"I can see that," McDermott said in his reedy voice.

I moved the front sheet of paper to the back, uncovering my next message: "YOU SAVED MY LIFE." It seemed like such a trite thing to say, but it needed saying.

"You're very welcome."

I shuffled my papers. "FOR AN OLD GUY WHO'S BEEN IN A GUNFIGHT, YOU LOOK PRETTY GOOD."

He smiled. I had written the comment before I had seen him, and of course he knew it.

I held up, "YOU SHOULD SEE THE OTHER GUYS."

A spasm of pain crossed his face. "I heard they were all dead," he said.

Brooke said, "One of them's going to make it, they think, but nobody's been able to talk to him yet."

"I've never...killed..." He had to stop, interrupted by a weak spasm of coughing.

I hadn't written any messages to cover that one, so I reached out to put a hand on his arm. Then, on impulse, I bent over and kissed him on his forehead.

He smiled up at me. "Now that makes it worthwhile," he said.

We were standing in the corridor, waiting for the elevator, when the phone in my purse rang. I fished it out and handed it to Brooke.

"Hello?" she said. She held the phone against her chest, and said to me, "It's Detective Jordan. He wants to know where we are."

I nodded at her.

"Okay I should tell him, or okay he wants to know?"

I made a twirling motion with my index finger.

"Okay I should tell him?"

I nodded.

A moment later, she had the phone pressed to her chest again. "He's here, too. In the main lobby."

Again I nodded.

"Okay he's here, or okay we'll meet him?"

I rolled my eyes.

"Okay." Into the phone she said, "Stay put. We'll find you."

The elevator doors opened on the lobby, and there he was. Jordan wasn't leaving much to chance.

"Don't you look awful," he said to me.

I grimaced at him.

"Out of the frying pan, and into the fire."

I waved my hand to indicate he should say what he had to say, and he looked at Brooke.

"Can't she talk?"

"Not at all."

He grinned, and I could have smacked him. "Why don't we have a seat over here?" he said, motioning to some chairs. "Since the mouthpiece is out of commission, I guess I'll have to do most of the talking."

We sat.

"That was telephone wire they tied you with."

I raised my eyebrows.

"It matches the cord that was used on Wendy Walters, which supports your conspiracy theory." He squinted at my throat. "Boy, it does do damage, doesn't it?"

I couldn't say anything to that, but such a vacuous observation merited some kind of response, so I crossed my eyes at him.

He laughed. "Okay, okay, I'll get to the point. I spoke to Ian Maxwell, who spoke to the D.A. They're not going to try to indict your boyfriend…" He hesitated. "Was John Parker your boyfriend, or were you just blowing smoke in there?"

"Oh, they were lovers," Brooke said. "Big time."

I turned a disbelieving stare on her.

"Sorry," she said.

Jordan said, "And they're not going after you either. They could, of course. If it wasn't you or John Parker, then whoever killed Wendy Walters didn't leave fingerprints or anything else to indicate they'd ever been in the apartment."

"The telephone wire," Brooke said.

"Well, yes, the telephone wire. Anyway, the D.A.'s exercising his prosecutorial discretion and declining to prosecute." He had more to say, but I didn't pay much attention to it. As I was to discover over the next couple of days, conversation loses a lot of its appeal when you yourself can't contribute to it.

That was Wednesday. On Thursday, The Wall Street Journal carried a front-page article on McCormack Labs. The SEC was launching an investigation. Odyssey's brokerage arm had changed its recommendation from "Strong Buy" to "Sell," and the stock, which had closed at 62¼ the previous Friday, had dropped below 45.

I didn't go into work the rest of the week, and John handled my one court appearance that couldn't be rescheduled. On Friday evening, he showed up at my front door with a dozen roses.

"I never thanked you properly for everything you did for me," he said, holding out the flowers.

I came out onto the front stoop, but hesitated before taking them. I could forgive John Parker, could wish all the best for him, but the romantic spark was gone.

"You look good," he said. "Are you going out?"

I was wearing a short, blue-jean skirt and a striped top with spaghetti straps. My hair was in its usual ponytail, but I had put on makeup.

"Yes," I said. My voice still had a whispery quality, but it was audible.

"Who with?" He sounded so aggrieved that I had to laugh at him. A big Ford pickup pulled up to the curb, and John turned to frown at it. Dustin Steed, one of the workmen I had met outside Wendy's apartment, opened the door of the pickup and got out. He had looked me up, though it had taken him long enough to do it. Now he came up the sidewalk wearing Wranglers and a polo shirt.

"With him?" John said.

I smiled, tilting my head at him and giving him a shrug. "Hi," I said hoarsely to Dustin.

"Hi. Am I interrupting something?"

I was standing in the doorway with a dozen roses on one arm.

"No," I said. "Just give me a minute to put these in water."

I left the two of them together on the front stoop. When I came back, I couldn't tell that either had said a word to the other. "Well, see you," I said to John.

He watched us go. I let Dustin help me into his pickup, then looked back at John as Dustin walked around to the driver's side. John was sitting on the stoop watching us go, his forearms resting on his knees. His expression was glum, and I really did feel sorry for him.

Dustin got in and slammed his door. "You ready?"

I turned to smile at him. He had beautiful eyes, brown and warm. I didn't know if he was built like his friend Steve because I'd never seen him without his shirt, but he looked like he could be.

"What?" he said.

I shook my head to clear it of such avid speculations, and he started the truck.

"Sex never delivers all it promises, does it?" I said, and put a hand to my mouth. Once again, the filter between my brain and my mouth had let a big one through.

He took his hand off the gearshift and looked at me. "You were looking at me and thinking about sex? That's encouraging."

I moved my hand. "Sex, and how it never delivers all it promises."

"It delivers a lot."

"But it promises everything."

He waited, but I didn't follow up. He shrugged and put the truck in gear. Glancing out the window, I saw that John Parker hadn't moved from his position on the porch. "Have you ever had sex with anyone?" I asked Dustin.

He looked at me. "Boy, you get personal on a guy in a hurry, don't you?" He pulled away from the curb, turned the corner, added gas.

"Have you?"

"Yes."

"Were you in love?"

"Yes."

"It felt like forever, and you were content with that?"

He shrugged, glanced again at me. "Yes."

"Where is she now?"

After a minute or so he said, "I take your point." He turned onto the entrance ramp of I-64 and accelerated. "I guess this means I'm not getting any tonight, am I?" he said.

I laughed, and he shot a glance at me.

"Am I?"

ABOUT THE AUTHOR

Michael Monhollon took out a semester in college to write science fiction stories and collect rejection slips. His first book sale, a legal thriller, came at the age of 31 at about the time *The Firm* was coming out in paperback. Its sales fell short of *The Firm*'s, though, and he continues to work for a living. Currently, he is the dean of the Kelley College of Business at Hardin-Simmons University in Abilene, Texas.

www.ingramcontent.com/pod-product-compliance
Lightning Source LLC
Chambersburg PA
CBHW060856250626
47159CB00008B/2758